THE SECRET OF THE RED PEARL

REBBE MENDEL

PRESENTS

THE SECRET OF THE RED PEARL

by NATHAN STERNFELD

FELDHEIM PUBLISHERS
JERUSALEM NEW YORK

First published in Hebrew as
Rak Sheloshah Chodashim... by Rebbe Mendel (5763)

Illustrated by David Bichman
Translated into English by S. Wolfsohn
Edited by Deena Nataf

Also by the author:
Adventures with Rebbe Mendel (Jerusalem: Feldheim Publishers, 2002)
All About Motti and His Adventures with Rebbe Mendel (Jerusalem: Feldheim Publishers, 2004)

ISBN 1-58330-798-2

First published 2005
Copyright © 2005 by the author

FELDHEIM PUBLISHERS
POB 43163 / Jerusalem, Israel

208 Airport Executive Park
Nanuet, NY 10954

www.feldheim.com

10 9 8 7 6 5 4 3 2 1

Printed in Israel

Contents

THE SECRET OF THE RED PEARL

1
The Great Debate

Dear reader, do you know what an archaeologist is? An archaeologist is a person who digs in the ground or dives in the sea searching for ancient remains. Sometimes he finds gold, jewelry, or other treasure. More often, he finds ruins of buildings and things we would not even notice: pieces of broken pottery, bits of metal, scraps of cloth. But these can be more important to the archaeologist than any treasure, because they are remnants of the daily life of people who lived long, long ago. What the archeologist wants to find out is how these people lived, how they earned their living, what they ate, and so on. And sometimes an archaeologist finds something that was written by one of these people of long ago...

Every year, archaeologists gather from all over the world to discuss the latest findings and to hear what others have to say about controversial subjects. Two years ago, the congress was in Amsterdam, Holland. All the participants had waited impatiently for it to begin, because at that meeting there was going to be a hot debate on the question of whether or not a

1

gem called the Red Pearl actually existed somewhere in the world.

Among the participants was Professor Alain Petite-Sourie, director of the Archaeological Institute in Marseilles, France. He had always strongly insisted that somewhere there was such a gem. Professor Ludwig Steinbrecher of the Center for the Study of Precious Stones in Hamburg, Germany, was also attending the meeting. He, on the other hand, had maintained from the beginning that the Red Pearl didn't exist then, and never did.

And what about the rest of the participants in that year's conference? They had various opinions. Some supported Petite-Sourie, others supported Steinbrecher. A third group even held that there was once a Red Pearl, but that it no longer existed — and so there was no sense in looking for it.

*   *   *

Let us go now to that archaeological congress in Amsterdam.

At that very moment, the question of the Red Pearl came up for discussion. The chairman of the congress, the aged Dr. Gustav von Holzwald, rang a little bell on the chairman's desk. Everyone became quiet.

"As you all know, we have gathered on this important day to hear two esteemed scientists give opinions regarding the Red Pearl," said old Dr. von Holzwald emotionally. "For the benefit of the many guests who have joined us, I will summarize briefly the events that brought us to discuss this most unusual subject.

"Nearly three years ago, our colleague Dr. Raphael Bloch, director and head curator of the Maritime Museum in Haifa, Israel, found an urn buried in the sea floor between Haifa and Akko." Everybody turned toward Bloch, who was easily recognized because of his black yarmulke.

The chairman waited a moment and then continued. "In the urn were found ancient manuscripts, written by a Canaanite 3,400 years ago — some time before the conquest of the Holy Land by Joshua.

"In one of the manuscripts, the writer says that he sent to Sidan — which is what the city of Sidon was called then — 'red and white pearls and much gold.' The question before us is: Is it at all possible that there really were red pearls?"

The hall was completely silent as Dr. von Holzwald paused to catch his breath. "If there weren't any red pearls, my dear colleagues, then did the writer of this manuscript make a mistake? Or did he exaggerate or lie? Or were they ordinary pearls that had been dyed red? As you are all aware, Professors Petite-Sourie and Steinbrecher disagree completely on this issue.

"And so, I am honored to invite these two great men to present their arguments. After that, we will continue with the other business of the congress."

The chairman sat down, and Alain Petite-Sourie, an enormous man with a thin, hoarse voice, stepped to the microphone — which had been raised almost a foot so that he would not have to bend down to speak.

"Gentlemen," began Petite-Sourie enthusiastically, "as you all know, pearls are made by living creatures called oysters.

The oysters we know today can produce only the whitish pearls we are familiar with. But isn't it possible that three thousand years ago there were other kinds of oysters as well — oysters that could make pearls of various colors? The answer is, Yes!"

When he said this, Petite-Sourie's thin voice turned into such a high squeak that the loudspeakers shrieked painfully for a long moment. After the noise and static from the microphone died down, the listeners once again heard Petite-Sourie's serious voice.

"It is certainly possible that there was a kind of oyster, which we may call the red oyster. And perhaps every last one of them has disappeared. Don't we read about animals that are in danger of extinction, or that have already become extinct? As scientists, we must have investigation and evidence. And the evidence is in the hands of Dr. Bloch: the manuscript in the Canaanite urn. Why should we suddenly suppose that the Canaanite writer lied — or that he was color-blind?"

Petite-Sourie paused to giggle at his own cute little remark. "Gentlemen, I wish to conclude my presentation. We have ancient testimony regarding the existence of red pearls. Therefore, I call upon all the archaeologists: Search, search carefully. It is clear to me that somewhere in the world there is at least one red pearl."

"Stuff and nonsense!" roared a voice from the middle of the auditorium.

Every head turned toward Ludwig Steinbrecher, the man who had interrupted Petite-Sourie's speech. Steinbrecher was

"Stuff and nonsense!" roared a voice from the middle of the auditorium.

so short that he had to stand on his chair in order to be seen. "Red pearls?" he yelled in a prodigious voice. "Absurd! What's your proof? Just the words of an ignorant Canaanite, who had some rubies and called them red pearls!"

"How dare you!" screamed Petite-Sourie in his high, squeaky voice, once again making the loudspeakers whistle. "First of all, speak when you are called upon to speak. Secondly, do you think the Canaanites didn't know the difference between rubies and pearls?"

Steinbrecher loudly answered from his place, "If in fact there were red pearls, then where are they now? What has become of them? Where did they go?"

"Where did they go?" yelled Petite-Sourie. "What business is that of mine? Look for them and you'll find them. They exist!" he screamed, and his face was red with rage.

"Your face, my friend Petite-Sourie," bellowed Steinbrecher, "is the only red pearl I know. You invent things and talk like a child!"

In the blink of an eye, Petite-Sourie's red face became as colorless as a white pearl, and he muttered, "No, this time I will not overlook it! He dares to ridicule me because I don't agree with him! No, no, I will not let it pass!" The immense Petite-Sourie was already pushing his way through the chairs toward Professor Steinbrecher, and if people hadn't stopped him and calmed him down, there is no doubt that he would have given the tiny German a good beating.

The chairman wrung his hands in anguish and cried, "Gentlemen, please! There are guests here. This is disgraceful!" Then he announced, "I will call on you, Professor Steinbrecher, to state your position, provided that you publicly apologize to Professor Petite-Sourie."

Steinbrecher approached the lectern. He was the complete opposite of his French colleague: short, but with a loud, strong voice.

The sound technicians ran to lower the microphone so that Steinbrecher could reach it, but the tiny scientist waved his hand in dismissal. "There is no need for loudspeakers," he roared, "but bring something for me to stand on!"

A stool was quickly brought and placed behind the lectern, and Steinbrecher mounted it. "Gentlemen," he said in a rush, "this is a monstrous outrage! Not one single marine scientist has ever spoken of an imaginary oyster that produces red pearls. "My respected colleague Professor Petite-Sourie — from whom I ask forgiveness for my outburst and for calling his face a red pearl — brings as proof of the existence of such an oyster a letter written by some doubtful Canaanite. But I, too, bring clear proof: If there were red pearls, then they would be found all over the world, decorating ancient jewelry and the like. Where are they? Show me just one red pearl! In summary, I say that the Red Pearl is a dream, a folly, a figment of the imagination."

No sooner had Steinbrecher finished speaking than the auditorium erupted in turmoil. Everyone was asserting his own opinion loudly and defending his own position.

Dr. Raphael Bloch, the director of the Haifa Maritime Museum and the man who had found the ancient urn, got up quietly and made his way to the exit. He had heard all he needed to hear. For him, this archaeological congress was over.

2
The Red Pearl

Dear reader, let us leave the controversy at the Amsterdam archaeological congress and move forward two years to the present day. We shall now meet one of the world's leading scientists, Dr. Ph. Litmus, of Brussels, Belgium.

By the time he was fifty years old, Litmus was a world-famous chemist, with dozens of important discoveries and inventions to his credit. He was convinced that he deserved the Nobel Prize for his contributions to science, and hoped to get it soon. (The Nobel Prize is named after Alfred Nobel, the Swedish chemist who invented dynamite. It is the highest honor a scientist can receive — and besides, the cash award is nothing to sneeze at.) But his hopes were in vain. Every year the prize was awarded to someone else, and with each year that passed, Litmus became angrier and more bitter.

When he turned sixty, Litmus was feeling pretty hopeless. He finally decided that if this time he didn't get the prize he so longed for, he would leave the world of science that had disappointed him so much and seclude himself in his house.

And that's just what happened. Litmus didn't get the Nobel Prize, and from the very day that the awards were announced, he shut himself in his house. He was furious at the whole world — but especially at the world of science. All that he wanted was to take revenge on scientists for not giving him the honor he felt he deserved.

About a month before this year's archaeological congress was scheduled to begin, Dr. Litmus read an article by Dr. Raphael Bloch in a leading science magazine. It was then that he remembered the controversy surrounding the Red Pearl. Suddenly, he had an idea. He smiled bitterly to himself and said with determination, "Ha! I'll cook that Bloch up a red pearl — and that'll be something interesting for him!"

Litmus immediately got to work. First, he mixed various chemicals in a large test tube (I can't tell you what they were, because it's a secret). Then, he boiled the mixture for a while. After that, he added another chemical to the test tube drop by drop, until the "soup" in the test tube suddenly changed color and became dark red.

Next, he let the mixture cool to room temperature and added a few grains of a certain powder. Then he let it stand for an hour and poured off the liquid, which had gradually become clear. There, nestled at the bottom of the test tube, was the result: a blood-red pearl almost an inch in diameter — a gigantic pearl, and red!

Litmus tipped the pearl into his hand, looked at it closely, and whispered, "I'm a genius, that's all there is to it! A red pearl, straight out of the kitchen, and on the first try, too!" He laughed, then said to himself, "It's so beautiful that it's really a shame it will last only three months before it melts.

"Now I'll send my 'pearl' to the museum in Haifa, and make Bloch and the whole scientific world look foolish. I would love to be at this year's congress and see old von Holzwald declare solemnly before the whole world that a new gem has been discovered — and then a couple months later have to admit publicly that the thing somehow mysteriously disintegrated and disappeared."

A few days later — but still some time before that year's congress was due to start — Litmus arranged for a special messenger to take the pearl to the Haifa Maritime Museum. When the messenger arrived, he insisted on speaking to the director.

Dr. Bloch showed the messenger — who, incidentally, looked a bit unusual in an elegant business suit covered with a red leather jacket — to a chair in his office and asked him his business.

"I represent a well-known European millionaire who wishes to remain anonymous," said the messenger. "Ever since you found the Canaanite urn, my employer has been very interested in the question of the Red Pearl.

"Recently, he was looking at some pieces of ancient jewelry in his collection. To his great surprise, he discovered a red gem that looks just like a pearl. He decided to send it to you for evaluation."

At this point, the strangely dressed man opened up a briefcase that was — inexplicably — dark blue. He extracted a small envelope and handed it to Dr. Bloch along with a piece of paper.

"Please sign this receipt. It confirms that you have the gem in your possession. You may call this number when you have completed your testing on the gem."

And with that, the messenger rose abruptly from his chair, turned, and left — leaving an openmouthed, speechless Dr. Bloch.

*   *   *

Ten minutes later, Dr. Bloch had recovered enough to place a phone call to Professor Ludwig Steinbrecher of the Center for the Study of Precious Stones in Hamburg, Germany.

*   *   *

Three weeks later, we find ourselves in Geneva, Switzerland, where this year's archaeological congress was being held. Dr. Gustav von Holzwald was about to bring the morning session to order. "Colleagues and friends," the chairman begun, "you might well remember the Amsterdam Congress two years ago. One of the sessions was devoted to a discussion — or rather, umm, a raging argument — regarding the existence of a gem called the Red Pearl."

The audience murmured in recognition as von Holzwald continued. "My esteemed colleagues, Dr. Raphael Bloch and Professor Ludwig Steinbrecher, have requested to present what they believe is incontrovertible evidence proving the existence of the Red Pearl."

The murmuring turned into a roar as Dr. Bloch and Professor Steinbrecher made their way to the lectern. Then

Bloch began to speak, and the hall became silent.

"As scientists, we all know that as long as there is no clear proof of the existence of the Red Pearl, it will be impossible to declare one way or the other if it indeed exists."

"However," Steinbrecher took over, his loud voice ringing through the hall, "unquestionable proof" — he paused dramatically and then finished — "exists!" He was silent for a moment and then declared dramatically, "We have in our possession a red pearl!"

The audience erupted. Bloch beckoned to two guards standing off to the side. They approached carrying a small safe and put it on the speaker's table. Bloch rotated the knob of the safe's combination lock this way and that, and then turned the handle and swung the door open. He reached into the safe and took out a small box of bulletproof glass. In the box, resting on a silk pillow, was a blood-red pearl almost an inch in diameter.

Bloch turned to the audience and said, "Gentlemen, I must admit that my personal opinion was like that of Professor Steinbrecher's. I thought that there was no such thing as a red pearl. Even now I am somewhat surprised to see one, because its existence contradicts some of the findings of my own research. When I first saw the pearl, I thought it must be a fake. But as I am an archaeologist and not a gemologist, I decided to contact Professor Steinbrecher.

"I have spent the past three weeks in Hamburg, Germany, with Professor Steinbrecher. After extensive testing, the Professor has declared this gem to be a genuine red pearl.

"The pearl has been loaned for six months to the Haifa

Maritime Museum by its owner, who wishes to remain anonymous. Even I do not know his identity. It will be residing in a closed exhibit hall. Professor Steinbrecher and I will prepare an article describing the find and our rigorous testing of it. We hope to publish it in a leading science magazine."

The audience clapped as Dr. Bloch gave over the lectern to Professor Steinbrecher. The professor described at length the exhaustive testing process to which the gem had been subjected. When he concluded his remarks, he declared loudly, "There can be no doubt. This is a genuine red pearl."

Everyone in the hall clapped again when the chief opponent of the Red Pearl publicly announced his change of mind.

The chairman then said excitedly, "It is my pleasure to announce the existence of a gem that was unknown until now: the Red Pearl!"

The pearl itself was returned to the safe, and everyone came to congratulate Dr. Raphael Bloch and Professor Ludwig Steinbrecher.

* * *

In the balcony with the rest of the spectators sat the head of a gang of international criminals, a man known only as Big Ralph. Next to him sat his second-in-command, Panno.

"Panno," whispered Ralph, "take a good look at that Jew doctor, and find out everything you can about him."

"What for, boss?" Panno asked.

"What for? What are you asking 'what for' for?" whispered Big Ralph angrily. "We are about to go to Israel to take that rare pearl for ourselves." He quietly laughed in pleasure at the thought. Then he took out a small camera and began to photograph Raphael Bloch from every possible angle.

*   *   *

Back in Brussels, Dr. Ph. Litmus read in the newspaper about what had happened at the Geneva congress. He chuckled with satisfaction. He could not know that at that very moment, Big Ralph was mobilizing his gang in order to steal the "pearl" he had cooked up — the pearl that would melt and decompose in less than three months' time.

But if he had known, he would not have just chuckled; he would have rolled on the floor laughing until the tears streamed down his face and he had no breath left to laugh with.

3
At the Circus

T he audience cheered and clapped as Leo Fellini, the lion trainer, directed his big cats out of the ring.

"And now, ladies and gentlemen," announced the ringmaster in a thunderous voice, "I am proud to present the master magician and king of the conjurors, Gazlano the Great!"

The crowd roared, and the magician strode into the ring, performing one trick after another as he walked around the big circle bowing to the audience.

Everyone in the audience sat spellbound, their eyes following the magician's every movement — except for one man. This was Panno, Big Ralph's lieutenant. He took no interest in the performance, and was bothered by the noise of the crowd. Anyone who noticed him could see that. He was there only because his son — who was more than a little spoiled — had pestered him endlessly about going to the circus. He had finally agreed to take him only to get a little peace.

Panno may have been sitting in the audience, but his thoughts were far away, on the Red Pearl. So while the audience applauded the magician's tricks, Panno closed his eyes and tried to organize his thoughts. But no plan of action came to him.

Suddenly, there was loud clapping for some especially astonishing trick. Panno was annoyed. He tried to concentrate on the Red Pearl, but he couldn't. He felt someone shaking his arm, and his son, Jackie, said, "Dad, instead of thinking all the time, look a little. Oh wow! That's the twentieth egg he's taken out of his hat."

"You can look if you want to, but leave me alone," growled Panno. "There's not one of those stupid tricks that I don't know. Do you think he has a chicken in his hat laying eggs? His hat has a pocket with three or four eggs in it, except they're plastic eggs, so they can't break. Every time he takes one out he holds it up and then puts it back in his hat a second later when everyone is looking at something else."

At that moment, the magician turned to the audience and said, "Ladies and gentlemen, permit me to say in all due modesty that there is not a lock in the world that I cannot open within ten seconds. I would like a volunteer, someone who will let himself be locked up, so you will see for yourselves that no lock in the world is too difficult for Gazlano the Great."

"Dad," said Jackie, poking his father, "can I do it? Please!"

Panno, lost in thought, didn't understand just what his son wanted, so he said, "Yeah, okay," and only then added, "I mean — what do you want?" But the question came too late. Jackie shoved a camera into his father's hand, said, "Great! Take my picture, will you?" and was out of his seat and in the ring next to Gazlano the Great before his father knew what was happening. Panno, confused, stopped thinking about crime and looked at his son, who was smiling and enthusiastic.

Then he took a good look at Gazlano for the first time — and nearly fainted with shock. The man in the ring appeared to be none other than Dr. Raphael Bloch, the archaeologist!

"What's going on here?" thought Panno dizzily. "That trickster down there looks just like that Jew Dr. Bloch! Is someone going to tell me that Bloch works as a circus magician in his spare time?" He took a picture of the archaeologist out of his pocket and studied it closely. Then he looked at Gazlano the Great for a long moment, and then back at the picture. "No," he said to himself deliberately, "it's no mistake. The man in the picture and the one in the ring are identical — except Bloch has that little black cap on his head and Gazlano doesn't."

The magician smiled at Panno's son and announced, "Now, ladies and gentlemen, I am about to lock up — what's your name, my boy?"

"Jackie," answered the boy, a little embarrassed.

Instantly, Panno shook himself loose from his thoughts and became a father. "What's going on here? What did that clown in the ring say? That he was going to lock up my son? Who said he could?" Then he remembered that he himself had given his son permission to volunteer.

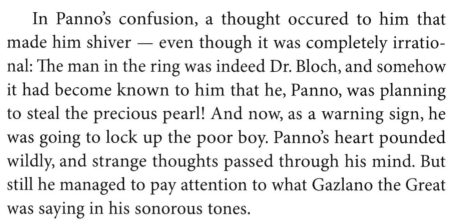

In Panno's confusion, a thought occured to him that made him shiver — even though it was completely irrational: The man in the ring was indeed Dr. Bloch, and somehow it had become known to him that he, Panno, was planning to steal the precious pearl! And now, as a warning sign, he was going to lock up the poor boy. Panno's heart pounded wildly, and strange thoughts passed through his mind. But still he managed to pay attention to what Gazlano the Great was saying in his sonorous tones.

"And so, ladies and gentlemen, first I will handcuff young Jackie, then lock him in a box made of unbreakable glass. The box is equipped with a special fan that will give Jackie air at all times. Next, I will lock the glass box in a safe, and then pass a long, heavy chain around the safe several times before locking that, too. Finally, with my assistant's help, I will put the safe into a heavy metal cabinet and my assistant will weld the door shut, and..."

"No, doctor!" exclaimed Panno, jumping to his feet. "Don't you dare do that, you heartless wretch! Would you kidnap a child because of your filthy pearl?"

The whole audience looked at Panno in astonishment, and Gazlano said, "I'm sorry, sir, but I am no doctor, and I don't know what pearl you are talking about." The confused Panno sat down sheepishly. He felt every eye on him.

The enthusiastic Jackie smiled broadly while Gazlano handcuffed him. With the assistant's help, Jackie climbed into the glass box, which the magician then locked with great show. He threw the keys to the handcuffs and the glass box far into the crowd, and then, with the help of his assistant, pushed the glass box into a large safe.

After closing the safe, spinning the combination knob with a flourish, and trying the handle vigorously, Gazlano the Great took a long chain, quickly passed it twice around the safe, and locked the two ends together with a heavy padlock. He pulled on the padlock several times to show the audience that it was securely locked, and then threw the padlock key into the audience as well. Finally, his assistant rolled the safe into a large, heavy metal cabinet and welded the door shut while the audience looked on.

"Within fifteen seconds, Jackie will be out, and his handcuffs off," declared Gazlano. Slowly and deliberately, he tied a thick handkerchief over his eyes. He took a thin steel wand out of his pocket and felt his way to the metal cabinet with the welded door.

Only four seconds were left, then three, then two... And then — so quickly that no one could see how it happened — the cabinet, the safe, and the glass box were all wide open — and Jackie climbed out smiling, his hands free.

The crowd cheered wildly, and Panno breathed a sigh of relief. "What an idiot I was," he thought. "Obviously, Gazlano is Bloch's twin brother — no two ways about it." He took five or six pictures of Gazlano with his son's camera and then rushed out to report his discovery to Big Ralph.

"Hey, boss, it's me, Panno," he said when Big Ralph answered the phone. "Can I ask you something about Dr. Bloch's family?"

"You can try," answered Ralph. "What do you want to know?"

Jackie climbed out smiling, his hands free.

"Does he have a twin brother?"

"He does," answered Ralph, "He has a twin who lives in the U.S., and he…"

"You don't have to tell me, boss," interrupted Panno. "He's a magician, and he performs with the Baldini Circus."

Panno heard Ralph laughing heartily at the other end of the line. "Have you gone crazy, Panno?" he finally said. "Bloch's twin is Rabbi Aharon Bloch, and he's the rabbi of a synagogue in a place called Monsey, in the United States."

"As far as I'm concerned, he can be a rabbit, not a rabbi," said Panno, "but in his spare time he's a circus magician."

"That's nonsense, Panno. You don't know what you're talking about. Jews don't even go to circuses, let alone perform in them! And you're trying to tell me that a well-known rabbi does tricks under the bigtop? Impossible!" He laughed again.

Panno was hurt by the way Big Ralph dismissed his information as worthless. "Well boss," he said, "then maybe you can explain how it is that I saw Dr. Bloch in the circus ring with my own eyes. Maybe they're triplets."

"No," said Ralph with finality. "Dr. Bloch has just one brother, his twin. Maybe this magician just looks very much like him. Did you take a picture?"

Panno said he had, and his boss said, "Good. Get the pictures developed and be at the Shack tonight at ten." Then he hung up.

4
The Plot

The Waterfront Shack was not on the waterfront and was not a shack. It was a very popular — and expensive — restaurant in downtown Cologne, Germany. Big Ralph, the owner, had spent a lot of money on the furnishings and decor so that the very fashionable guests could pretend that they were eating in a beachcomber's cabin on a Pacific island. It was from his office here that Big Ralph ran his criminal activities, but none of the restaurant's patrons knew that. Neither did the police.

As soon as Panno walked in, the headwaiter saw him. He came over quickly and ushered Panno past the swinging doors that led to the kitchen, and down the hall to the owner's office. As he opened the door, he told Panno that the boss was waiting for him.

Ralph was in the middle of a telephone conversation when Panno came in. "Okay, you said Gazlano's real name is Sigmund Kranker. He's the son of Peter and Irena Kranker, and he was born in Cologne in 1951. Did I get that right? Good. Thank you, Werner. Come by the Shack any evening and pick up what I promised you. If I'm not here, the head-waiter will know about it." Ralph put down the receiver and beckoned Panno to sit down.

"Tell me," he said coyly, "what was Dr. Bloch going to do to your son, that made you yell at him like that?" Ralph threw back his head and laughed.

Panno blushed when he was reminded of how alarmed he had been and how he yelled at the circus magician. "How do you know about that, boss?" he asked.

"How could I not know?" answered Ralph. "Look, the whole town is talking about the strange man who gave his son permission to be locked up by the magician — and then yelled at him and awarded him the title of doctor — but let's hear the whole story from the horse's mouth."

Panno recounted briefly what had happened at the circus, and then put three photographs of Gazlano on the desk. Next to them, he laid a photograph of Dr. Bloch.

"Unbelievable!" Ralph murmured. "It really could be the same person. The only difference is the yarmulke — that's the little black beanie, Panno."

"So, boss, now do you understand why I was so sure he was Bloch's twin brother?"

"Of course. But they're not twins. They're not even related. Dr. Bloch and his twin, Rabbi Bloch, were born in 1950 in the United States. Their parents were Shlomo and Chaya Bloch. That's on record in the town where they were born. Sigmund Kranker — Gazlano the Great — isn't even Jewish. He was born in 1951 in Germany. That's the information I got from the fellow I was talking to on the phone when you came in. I don't know how he finds things out, but he's never wrong."

"If that's true," said Panno, "then they're doubles!"

"That's the right word, Panno. I don't know if it's true, but I once read that every person has a double somewhere in the world, and that a person and his double are alike as two drops of water — even though they aren't related."

The two were silent for a moment. Suddenly Ralph sat up straight, banged his fist on the desk, and exclaimed, "We are idiots!"

"What are you talking about, boss?" asked Panno, surprised.

"If this Sigmund Kranker really is a magician and an expert at picking locks, and on top of that is a perfect double for Bloch, then..."

"Then what?" prompted Panno.

"Don't you understand?" exclaimed Ralph. "Listen carefully and you will. We offer Kranker a good price to work for us. We go to Israel, kidnap Dr. Bloch, and have Kranker stand in for him. That way, we have one of our people as the director of the museum. He'll soon find out where the pearl is kept. Then, since he's so good with his hands, it'll be easy for him to steal the Red Pearl and replace it with a red porcelain bead. Then he'll just pass the Red Pearl along to one of our people."

"That's a great idea, boss," said Panno.

"Of course it is, Panno. Why do you think I'm the boss, and not you? Okay, you can go now. Go see this Sigmund Kranker fellow tomorrow. The Baldini Circus is based here in Cologne. Feel him out carefully and see if he's willing to talk about a deal. If he is, arrange a meeting."

*   *   *

Panno had done his job well. He arranged a meeting between Sigmund Kranker and Ralph. Two days had now passed since Ralph proposed to Kranker that he stand in for Dr. Raphael Bloch for a few days. Kranker had not yet answered.

His first thought was to reject the offer out of hand: "Why should a person who has been honest all his life suddenly break the law? Should I become a criminal and a gangster just for money?"

But as Kranker looked again and again at the photograph of Dr. Bloch that he had been given, the turmoil in his heart grew. He didn't know why, but he was drawn to this adventure — to be Dr. Bloch for a few days — as if by mysterious cords. Inexplicably, he felt that something very strong connected him to the name Bloch — and he wondered whether this feeling had something to do with his childhood.

Then his conscience cried out, "No! A thousand times no! I will not become a common criminal!"

His conscience said No, his intelligence said No — but his feelings said Yes. He felt like a swimmer being dragged down by a powerful current — down, down, into the depths. He simply had to be Dr. Bloch for those few days. He didn't want any part of the crime, but finally his decision was — yes.

*   *   *

A few days later, Big Ralph and Sigmund Kranker reached an agreement, and the next day they met to complete their plans. After all of the details had been settled, Sigmund said, "There are two things I have to tell you. First of all, I want to be sure that no harm will come to Dr. Bloch. You have to promise me that."

"What difference does that make to you?" asked Big Ralph.

"What do you care if it makes a difference to me? He's my double, not yours.

"The other thing is this: I know that once that pearl is in your hands, you won't have any reason not to cheat me or even harm me. For that reason, I have left a letter in my safe deposit box in my local bank. The letter has all the details of our agreement, and I've given my bank manager instructions to open the box and give the letter to the police if I'm not back within four months. That way, I won't have to worry about your harming me — because, after all, you won't want that letter to reach the police."

"You think of everything," said Ralph.

"Yes, that's true, and that's why I'm not the leader of a miserable gang of crooks."

Ralph turned red with rage, but Panno — who was at the meeting — smiled with pleasure. He was happy that Ralph was feeling the way the members of his gang felt when he humiliated them.

The operation was scheduled to start in a month's time, and Sigmund spent most of it studying Hebrew intensively. He realized that being a magician was standing him in good stead, as he was used to memorizing tricks, sequences of cards, people's faces, etc. Sigmund felt as if a strange force were guiding him, putting the pieces of a puzzle into place for him. But he couldn't understand the puzzle. He felt, however, that once again it had something to do with his past...

When the day came to fly to Israel, Sigmund was confident that his command of Hebrew was more than good enough. He just hoped that he would be able to effect Dr. Bloch's American accent when speaking his new language. At least he spoke English like an American. He had always had an uncanny gift for English, but could never figure out why it came so easily to him. When Sigmund learned it in high school, his teacher couldn't get over how quickly and fluently he had learned to both read and speak it.

All this time, dear reader, the clock was ticking, and on the very day that Sigmund flew to Israel, the Red Pearl was two months old. In other words, there were less than thirty days left before the pearl would disintegrate and disappear.

5
Three Peas in a Pod

Yosef Bloch's room looked like it was a week before Pesach. Clothes were scattered everywhere, and his mother was patiently packing them into suitcases.

Yosef — or Yossi, as he was usually called — was Rabbi Aharon Bloch's oldest son, and he was as excited as could be. This was the first time that he was going to visit his uncle Rafi in Israel by himself. Uncle Rafi's wife, Aunt Minna, had gone to California with the kids for the summer, in order to visit her parents. Yossi had grabbed the opportunity to keep his beloved uncle company — and, of course, to learn Torah in the Holy Land as well.

Yossi was sixteen years old, but he felt like a little boy; every time he thought about the trip, he got butterflies in his stomach.

"Uncle Rafi will be waiting for you at the airport," his mother said for the millionth time. "You remember what he looks like, don't you?"

"Of course I do, Imma," he answered. "He comes here

a lot, and the last time we were all there was just two years ago. Besides, he and Abba are alike as two peas in a pod. All I have to do when I get off the plane is look for someone who looks just like Abba, except without the beard."

"You're right," Yossi's mother said. "Abba and Uncle Rafi really are alike as two peas in a pod."

At that moment Yossi's father passed the door to the room. He stopped in the doorway, sighed, and said, "That's not quite true. Actually, we are alike as three peas in a pod."

"What do you mean, Abba, three peas in a pod?" asked Yossi, frowning in puzzlement.

Rabbi Bloch sighed again. "If two people look very much like each other, we say they are alike as two peas in a pod. If three people look alike, then they have to be alike as *three peas in a pod.*"

"Aharon," said his wife, "why must you talk about such painful matters?"

But Rabbi Bloch said firmly, "The time has come for Yosef to know. That way, Moishy will not be forgotten."

"Abba," said Yossi, confused, "who is Moishy? And who are the three look-alikes?"

"It's a long story," said Yossi's father. "May I come in and sit down?" Yossi nodded and his father sat down at the desk, while Yossi seated himself on his bed. Rabbi Bloch's voice shook a little as he began to tell the story.

"I was born a triplet, and not a twin, as you always thought. There were articles about us in the newspapers, and our parents even got a special grant from the state. In those days, the birth of healthy, normal triplets was a rare thing.

"We resembled each other so much that we ourselves sometimes couldn't tell who was who of the other two. I remember to this very day times I called one of my brothers Rafi, when in fact it was Moishy, and vice versa. But even though we looked alike, we were very different from each other in our personalities. I was a normal child, not outstanding or unusual in any way. On the other hand, from the time he could walk, Rafi was a collector. He had a million collections — butterflies, leaves, autographs of famous people. He even had a fingerprint collection."

"A fingerprint collection?" asked Yossi in amazement.

"Yes, believe it or not, a fingerprint collection. I remember when for an *afikomen* present he asked for a bottle of the special ink that's used for taking fingerprints. When he got it, he went out and bought a small notebook and we all had to leave our fingerprints in it. First Rafi took his own fingerprints, then Moishy and I had to let him take ours. After that, he took fingerprints from our parents, aunts, uncles, cousins, and even the neighborhood storekeepers. Unless I am mistaken, your uncle Rafi still has that book."

"And what was Moishy like?" asked Yossi eagerly.

"Moishy was an adventurer," said his father with another sigh. "He dragged us along on all sorts of expeditions, especially in the summers when we rented a bungalow in the Catskill Mountains. He would often take us to wild and desolate places. He loved dangerous adventures, and Rafi and I, to our sorrow, didn't tell our parents about them. We thought that would make us 'informers.' Now we know that if we had told our parents, his life might have been saved."

Yossi's father took a deep breath and continued. "In the middle of the summer that we were 10 years old, Moishy ran into the house one day flushed and out of breath and exclaimed, 'Aharon, Rafi, come with me! You have to!' Rafi was pasting a dried leaf in an album, and I was learning.

"We looked at Moishy's sweaty face, and I asked him what he had found this time. He answered, 'Mr. Smith's lost donkey!' Mr. Smith was an elderly man who used to go from bungalow colony to bungalow colony giving rides to the children in a cart that was pulled by a donkey. But the donkey had run away a few days before. Moishy was determined to help Mr. Smith find the donkey, as it was the older man's only means of *parnassah*.

"Rafi and I asked Moishy where he had found the donkey. He said, 'On Wet Mountain.' Wet Mountain is what all the children in the bungalow colony called a certain steep, high hill that was situated next to a river. It had a small spring right at its top. The water from the spring didn't run down in a stream, but spread out, so the whole top of the hill was covered with slippery wet grass and mud.

"Moishy told us that he had climbed to the top of the hill. Rafi interrupted him. 'You went all the way to the top?' he said. 'Don't you know how dangerous that mud and wet grass is? You could slip and fall down into the river!' Moishy dismissed Rafi's fears with a wave of his hand. 'So listen,' he said, 'Smith's donkey is on the top of the hill, eating the grass, but it wouldn't be hard to tie a rope around its neck and lead it back to town.' Then Moishy ran off to the caretaker's shed and borrowed a long rope.

"It still brings tears to my eyes," continued Rabbi Bloch, "to think of how we let Moishy talk us into climbing that hill, when what we should have done was keep him from going.

"He took us up Wet Mountain on a path that he knew, and it was easy enough until we got close to the top. There, everything was wet and slippery from the nearby spring, and Moishy warned us to be careful and to always hold on to something solid. We held on for dear life to the rocks that stuck out of the ground, and to bushes that grew here and there. We looked fearfully down at the long, steep slope that led down to the river. Looking up, we saw Mr. Smith's donkey, surefootedly walking around the hilltop, grazing happily on the lush grass.

"Moishy was holding on to a rock, and I was right next to him. 'This is far enough, Moishy,' I said. 'It's dangerous. We'll never be able to reach the donkey. Let's go back before we slip and fall into the river. Look how high we are!' Rafi also thought we should go back. 'It's crazy to do something so dangerous for a donkey,' he said. 'We'll just tell Mr. Smith that his donkey is here, and be done with it.' Moishy answered contemptuously, 'Fine, go back if you want to. I've got a good hold on this rock, and I've made it to the top before.' Rafi and I looked at each other, perplexed. We couldn't think of any way to persuade stubborn Moishy to come with us.

"And then… then there was a terrible scream — Moishy screaming — a scream that rings in my ears to this very day. I was right next to him, so I saw what happened. A bee had stung him on his cheek, right by his eye, and because of the sudden, unexpected pain, he screamed and let go of the rock.

Because of the sudden, unexpected pain, Moishy screamed and let go of the rock.

I can't bear to tell what happened. Moishy slid and tumbled down the hill and then fell off the bank into the river — and disappeared!

"We never found Moishy — alive or dead. Of course, the police were informed, and the river was dredged. But they didn't find anything. My parents — your Saba and Savta — hired divers, but they didn't find anything, either. Only Moishy's yarmulke was found, at the edge of the river about a mile downstream from where he fell in. Moishy himself had disappeared.

"I still dream about him, and every time I do, the dream is the same. First, he appears, and says accusingly, 'Why? Why? Why did you let me do it?' Then he disappears in fog, and then I hear that same terrible scream."

Yossi sat transfixed, biting his lips with tension as the terrible secret of Moishy's disappearance was revealed to him. He pondered what he had heard for a moment and then said, "That means, Abba, that you never found proof that Moishy — really, my Uncle Moishy — isn't alive."

"That's true, though it is very unlikely that he is."

"But Abba, maybe he's alive after all!" exclaimed Yossi. "Doesn't Rashi bring a *midrash* in *Parashas Vayeishev* that says that because Yosef was still alive, Yaakov couldn't forget him? Maybe the reason you can't forget Moishy is that he is still alive somewhere."

"Maybe." Rabbi Bloch sighed deeply. "If only it were so."

*   *   *

At that very moment, far away in Europe, Gazlano the Great was in the circus ring, performing tricks that left his audience breathless. He was giving an especially brilliant performance, because this was his last appearance before flying to Israel.

6

At the Airport

The airplane carrying Yossi Bloch touched down at Ben Gurion International Airport in Israel. Twenty minutes later, after having his passport stamped and collecting his luggage, Yossi found himself one of the unlucky ones chosen at random to have his suitcases inspected. He therefore remained for several extra minutes standing at the "green line."

Ten minutes after Yossi's plane had landed, one from Cologne, Germany, had arrived. Among its passengers were Sigmund Kranker, also known as Gazlano the Great, and six "soldiers" from Big Ralph's gang. The seven men split up at passport control.

Kranker had sped through Passport Control and Baggage Claim, and so was on his way out of the arrivals terminal when Yossi was just placing his suitcases on the inspector's table. Thus it happened that Kranker, making his way to the exit, passed close by Yossi, who at that very moment turned his head. The eyes of the two met.

Kranker stopped, certain that he had seen the young man

before. Once again, he had the familiar feeling that he was on the verge of remembering something, that if he only tried harder he could push through the blanket of thick fog that concealed a memory.

All of this took less than a second, and then Kranker continued on his way. Yossi called after him, "Uncle Rafi! Uncle Rafi!" But when he saw that the man he thought was his Uncle Rafi didn't stop, he left his luggage on the table and hurried after him. He caught up with him and said, "Uncle Rafi, it's me, Yossi! Don't you recognize me?"

Kranker understood immediately what had happened. His face became pale for a moment, but he made an effort and succeeded in smiling. He said, "I have to move my car! I parked it illegally." He pointed to one of the exits and added, "Meet me outside that door there."

With those words, Kranker hurried toward the exit. He turned left, away from the parking lot, and entered the departures terminal — the designated meeting place for the gang. He hoped he could stay there until the young man who thought he was his uncle left the terminal.

Yossi had a strange feeling as he watched his uncle walk away. Then he noticed a group of six men walking quickly after him. "I don't know why, but that makes me suspicious," he thought. "It looks as if those six fellows are following Uncle Rafi. When we meet outside, I'll mention it to him."

In the meantime, the man inspecting Yossi's luggage started yelling at him to come back, take his suitcases, and get out of the terminal. Yossi hurried back to his suitcases, collected them, apologized to the inspector, and then ran to the exit. But when he finally got outside, he didn't see his uncle.

While Yossi was looking for his uncle, Kranker had gathered his six henchmen around him. "Gentlemen, this business is getting complicated. I don't know if you noticed, but I spoke briefly with a young man in the terminal," he said. "He is apparently a relative of Dr. Bloch's, and has come to visit him. His being here might seriously interfere with our plans."

In the meantime, Yossi was getting worried. He had looked everywhere without finding any sign of either his uncle or the six suspicious characters. While he was wondering what could have become of Uncle and what he should do, he heard a familiar voice calling, "Yossi! Yooossi!"

He looked in the direction of the voice and was relieved to see his uncle waving to him in greeting. But what had happened to Uncle Rafi all of a sudden? Did he think it was Purim today? Ten minutes earlier he had been wearing a plaid jacket and a tweed cap and carrying a leather briefcase, and now he was dressed altogether differently — a dark suit, a white shirt with a tie, and a gray felt hat. And instead of the briefcase, he carried his car keys.

Yossi had taken only a few steps before his uncle reached him and gave him a big hug.

"So, how are you?" the uncle asked his nephew. "You already look like quite the prince. Cubs become bears, and I — well, the bears grow older."

On the way to the car, Yossi and Uncle Rafi exchanged family news. Yossi was perplexed at the sudden change in his

What had happened to Uncle Rafi all of a sudden? Now he was dressed altogether differently.

uncle's dress. His curiosity grew from moment to moment, until, when they reached the car, he couldn't contain himself, and…

"Uncle Rafi, I'm confused," said Yossi.

"What's confusing you, my boy?" asked Uncle Rafi, opening the car and helping Yossi put his suitcases into the trunk. Yossi didn't know how to answer.

They got into the car, and after Uncle Rafi started it and they were on their way, he asked Yossi again why he was confused. "Is there something you don't understand?" he asked.

"Yes, there is!" answered Yossi. "When I first saw you inside the terminal, you were wearing completely different clothes. Then suddenly you disappeared. After that you appeared again, in the clothes you're wearing now. But there's no sign of the clothes you wore first or of the briefcase you were carrying then. Did you have to disappear because of those six suspicious-looking fellows? Is that the reason?"

Uncle Rafi glanced at his nephew briefly and said with a smile, "I see you managed to dream a lot during your flight. I wasn't even in the terminal building. And as for my clothes, I've been wearing them since the morning."

"What?!" burst out Yossi. "Didn't I talk to you in the terminal building? You said we would meet outside."

"Yossi, Yossi, please! It must have been a dream," said Uncle Rafi with finality. "Tell me more about what's happening in Monsey."

Yossi saw that his uncle didn't believe him, and he felt wounded. After all, he knew that he hadn't been dreaming. Nevertheless, he decided not to talk about the strange matter anymore. But then he remembered the six suspicious-looking men, and he said, "There is something I should tell you about anyhow. I think there were some men following you, and they didn't have pleasant faces."

"What you've just told me may well be true. I've been warned that there are probably all kinds of people who would be very happy to have the Red Pearl."

"What are you doing about it?" asked Yossi apprehensively.

"'He who trusts in God will be encircled by loving-kindness,'" answered his uncle.

*   *   *

That evening, Rafi Bloch told his nephew the story of the Red Pearl from the beginning, including the part about the messenger from the mysterious millionaire. "Tomorrow, you can come with me to the museum, and I'll show you the pearl."

After that, Yossi wanted to hear everything Uncle Rafi knew about his lost brother Moishy.

After listening to stories about his Uncle Moishy for over an hour, Yossi said, "I'm positive that he is alive. Eventually we will find him."

"Yes, yes," sighed Uncle Rafi. "I, too, dream that we will find him. I haven't stopped dreaming about him from the day he disappeared." Dr. Bloch got up and left the room for a moment. When he came back, he was carrying photographs, some notebooks, and a small, old yarmulke — Moishy's yarmulke, the one he was wearing when he tumbled into the river and disappeared — the one that was later found on the riverbank.

Yossi studied the photographs for a long time. In them could be seen happy triplet boys.

After that, Rafi showed him the notebooks. The first was filled with fingerprints. "Here," said Uncle Rafi, pointing to rows of what looked to Yossi like nothing but black smudges, "the first row are my fingerprints, the second row are Moishy's, and the third row are you father's." He opened another notebook and said, "These are Moishy's *chiddushei Torah*, and this last one is his 'tricks' notebook. Moishy was very clever with his hands. He used to make up magic tricks and record them in this notebook."

Yossi looked at the notebooks and then turned back to the photographs. He pointed to a framed photograph that showed three boys about nine years old standing next to a snowman. His uncle smiled and said, "This picture is special. It's the first one that was taken with the camera that our parents — your Saba and Savta — had just bought. So they had three extra prints made, one for your father, one for Moishy, and one for me. As a matter of fact, I had another print made of this recently, and hung it up in my office. You'll see it tomorrow when we're there."

Yossi was absorbed in studying the photographs and notebooks until very late. But he couldn't bring himself to touch the yarmulke. It was for him a silent witness to an overwhelming tragedy.

7

Peter and His Wife

Dear reader, let us now go back across the ocean, to the place where Yossi's Uncle Moishy disappeared — and back thirty-three years, to that very day.

Peter Kranker picked up his fishing rod and the battered basket with his other fishing gear and walked down to where his rowboat was tied up. He stepped into the boat, cast off the line, and, using an oar, pushed the boat into the current. He let the boat drift down the river while he lit a cigarette. His eyes wandered over the river's banks. On his left were woods thick with undergrowth, and on his right the high hill that the children called Wet Mountain. This part of the river had been nearly fished out by the tourists, and Peter never caught very much. But the sight of the little river running through hills dark with trees reminded him of the German countryside where he had grown up, and it made him happy to be there even if he came back empty-handed.

Suddenly Peter's eye was caught by a donkey standing near the top of the hill. He stood up in the boat to get a better look at the strange sight, and his heart clenched with dread when he saw three boys trying to reach the donkey, holding on to rocks and branches to make their way up the muddy hillside. The boys were high above the river, and Peter wanted to shout to warn them that they were in danger. But before he could open his mouth, he heard a horrific scream, and saw one of the boys sliding and tumbling down the steep, slippery slope, faster and faster, until he flew off the bank at the bottom of the hill and plunged into the river.

The boy disappeared into the water, but after a few seconds bobbed to the surface, bleeding heavily from a gash on his head. Then the current carried him swiftly downstream, unconscious.

Peter stood paralyzed with shock for a second. Then he tore off his shirt and shoes and dived into the water.

*　　　*　　　*

Irena Kranker, Peter's wife, was watering her flower beds. She and Peter lived in a cottage far from any neighbors. Although their house was small, it was large enough for them — because, to their sorrow, they had no children.

Suddenly she heard Peter shouting. "Light the stove! Quick!" She looked up and saw her husband rushing toward the house with a child in his arms. She hurried into the house and lit the stove. Peter came in and carefully put the unconscious child on his bed. Then he stood looking at him with pity. "It took so long!" he said. "It seemed like I gave him artificial respiration for half an hour before he began to breathe."

Irena looked at the blood-soaked rag wrapped around the boy's head. "I'd better change that," she said. When she took the rag off, she saw the deep gash in the boy's head. She quickly brought a towel with ice cubes in it, and held it on the cut until the bleeding stopped. Then she put on a clean bandage.

Suddenly, the boy started making strange gurgling noises. Peter pressed the boy's belly again and again, until he vomited all the water he had swallowed.

When Peter and his wife were sure that the boy was out of danger, Peter put him on the bed in the spare room and covered him with blankets.

"I recognize him," he said. "He's one of the triplets from the Jewish bungalow colony."

"Yes," sighed Irena. "They had three children born all at once, and we don't even have one."

She looked at the sleeping boy with pity and yearning. "How long do you think he'll sleep?" she asked her husband.

"I hope not more than twelve hours. If after twelve hours he doesn't wake up, we'll have to take him to the hospital," Peter answered knowledgeably. "But that won't be our problem, because I'm going right now to tell his parents that their son is here."

"Don't, Peter!" pleaded Irena, crying. "Think for a minute. It would be much better for the boy if we kept him. Everyone hates the Jews, and they are always suffering. With us…." She didn't finish the sentence, but then added, "Besides, we would raise him as a good Catholic."

Peter shook his head. "I'm a fisher of fish, not of souls. Besides, this argument is silly. As soon as the boy opens his eyes, he'll want to go home. Do you think you can force him to be your son? To keep him here against his will would be kidnapping."

"Oh, Peter, please!" she cried, then continued more calmly. "At least promise me that you won't say a word until the boy wakes up, and then we'll ask Father Pancreas."

Irena cried and begged, until Peter finally agreed to his wife's demand.

At that very moment, there was a knock. Irena closed the door to the room where the boy was sleeping behind her and went with Peter to open the front door.

She opened it. A policeman stood in the doorway. "That boat there," he said, pointing to where Peter's rowboat was tied up by the river, "is it yours?"

"Yes, it is," answered Peter.

"Were you out on the river today? Did you happen to hear anyone shouting for help, or see a boy in the water?"

Peter didn't answer. Irena said, "My husband has been in the house all day, and we didn't hear any shouts. What happened?"

"One of the children from the bungalow colony fell into the river and disappeared," answered the officer. "If you see or hear of anything, please inform the police immediately."

"Of course," said Irena, and the policeman left.

A few hours later, the boy woke up. He was burning with fever and dripping with sweat and mumbled incomprehensibly. After two days, he got over the fever, but he seemed

"We didn't hear any shouts. What happened?"

confused and couldn't take care of himself. When two more days had passed, it was clear to Peter and Irena that the boy didn't know who he was or where he came from.

At that point, Irena immediately called Father Pancreas. The priest came without delay, and as soon as Peter had finished explaining to him what had happened, he began to tell Peter how great a deed he would be doing by keeping the boy and raising him as a Catholic.

Peter knew perfectly well that what he ought to do was take the boy back to his parents, but he was subjected to an endless harangue by Father Pancreas. The good priest described in great detail the blazing fires of Gehinnom that would await Peter if he allowed the boy to go back to being a Jew — a word that he spat out as if it were dirt in his mouth.

Whenever Peter raised an objection, the priest started over again. And whenever Father Pancreas paused for breath, Irena began to wail and whimper about how they had been given a child at long last, and how she would die of sorrow if they didn't keep the boy.

With a heavy heart, Peter finally agreed, but he told his wife and the priest that he saw no way to keep it from becoming known that they had the boy — and then the police would be back and they would be charged with kidnapping.

"Of course, of course," said Father Pancreas, "you're absolutely right. That just means that you cannot stay in the United States. My idea is that you will go back to Germany — after all, that's where you were born and raised. I will see to getting the necessary papers.

"I'm going now, to get the ball rolling, but I'll be back in two or three days. In the meantime, stay in the house as much as possible, and above all, don't let anyone in." With that, he left.

Two days later, Father Pancreas was back with a birth certificate from a West-Coast city for Sigmund Kranker. (Sigmund was the name Irena decided to give Moishy.) When Peter stammered, "What…? How…?" the priest smiled secretively, waved his hand vaguely, and told Peter that he didn't have to know everything. He took care of Sigmund the next day while Peter and Irena went into the big city to apply for passports, and visited them almost every day until the passports came in the mail. Then he told them to be packed and ready to go at midnight.

On the stroke of midnight, Father Pancreas arrived. He bundled the Krankers into his car and drove straight through the rest of the night. At noon the next day, they arrived at a distant city that had direct flights to Germany. There, he left them in a motel and immediately set out to make the arrangements for their trip. Two days later, Peter and Irena Kranker, their "son" Sigmund, and the priest were flying over the Atlantic, bound for Germany.

And so, with the help of Father Pancreas, Peter and Irena Kranker and their adopted son Sigmund moved to Cologne, Germany. The priest stayed a few days to help them get settled and to obtain all the necessary forged documents he felt would be needed by the Krankers. He also bribed a junior clerk in the local office in charge of birth and death records to add a form to the file. On the form, it was recorded that a son named Sigmund was born to Peter and Irena Kranker in 1951.

As he was saying good-bye to Peter and Irena, Father Pancreas took a bulging manila envelope out of his briefcase and gave it to Peter, saying, "These are all the official documents you will need in connection with your new son, including school records and a copy of his German birth certificate. Study them carefully, so you will know what to say to him when the time comes. As far as other people are concerned, you moved to Cologne from Hamburg." When Peter opened his mouth to speak, the priest said with irritation, "As I told you before, there are things you don't have to know. All you do have to know is that you are earning yourselves a great reward in the World to Come by raising this boy as a Catholic."

Father Pancreas returned to the United States and made his way to the town where the Bloch triplets were born. There, just as in Cologne, he bribed a clerk to tamper with the birth records. He simply had the clerk remove and destroy the original of Moshe Bloch's birth certificate. Then he had the clerk modify Raphael and Aharon Bloch's birth certificates to read "twin" instead of "triplet."

Father Pancreas did his work very thoroughly. And now you can understand, dear reader, why Big Ralph's friend Werner was unable to uncover the connection between Dr. Bloch and Gazlano the Great.

8
Sigmund Suffers

Irena's happiness knew no bounds; finally, she had a child of her own! She spoiled Ziggy (that was the nickname they gave him) and gave him everything he wanted.

The Krankers only spoke to him in German. He was a bright boy, and picked up the language quickly. The blow to Moishy's-Ziggy's head had affected his memory, so his English was quickly forgotten before the neighbors had a chance to be suspicious. When Ziggy was finally able to understand an entire conversation in German, Irena explained to him that he had been sick for a long time with a dangerous illness and had been in a coma for six months. As a result, he had "forgotten" his German.

Irena tried to "remind" Ziggy of all sorts of things from his past — things from his childhood that of course had never really happened and that Irena had made up to suit her fancy. She repeated her stories over and over. Since Ziggy didn't remember anything about America, there was no question in his mind but that he had been born and raised in

51

Germany and had been an ordinary child in every way until he got sick. He understood that, although he had recovered from his illness, he had forgotten his past completely.

As much as Irena was happy, Peter and Sigmund were sad and depressed. Peter had terrible feelings of guilt, and Sigmund was preoccupied with his forgotten past. Something gave him no rest. He felt there was something in his past — something hidden by a thick fog of forgetfulness. Again and again, he felt that this time, now, he was going to remember a forgotten spark… and then, every time, the cloud of forgetfulness thickened and spread — and Sigmund was left frustrated and despairing.

"Mother," Ziggy asked Irena one day, "why didn't you take pictures of me when I was little? I don't even have one picture."

Irena looked at her "son," and her face became sad. "That's because of the fire," she said. "Ah, of course you don't remember the fire. Nine months ago, while you were sick, there was a fire in the house. Many books and papers were destroyed, as well as all the family pictures."

*   *   *

Once, Peter told his son that the next day they would go for a cruise on the Rhine. (The Rhine is a big and very beautiful river; Cologne, where the Krankers lived, is on the Rhine.)

Ziggy was excited about the outing. But the next day, when the boat pulled away from the dock and began to move into the current — and to rock gently back and forth

— Ziggy turned white, grabbed Peter's hand, and suddenly cried out, "Back! I want to go back to land!"

With the other passengers looking on curiously, Peter tried to calm his son. "What's wrong, Ziggy?" he asked. "Look at the beautiful view."

But Ziggy became even more pale, and his whole body began to shake. Sweat burst out on his forehead. "We're going to drown!" he screamed. "I want to get off!"

Peter felt he had no choice. He paid the owner of the boat a good sum of money to take them back to dry land immediately so that he and Sigmund could get off.

"What happened to you?" Peter asked when he saw that Sigmund had calmed down a little.

"I… I don't know," mumbled the boy. "I felt we were going to drown. I felt we were going to drown for sure. I can't explain why I felt that way."

"Poor child," said Peter, and hugged Sigmund. "Poor child!" Ziggy looked at his father and saw that his eyes were filled with tears. He realized that his father was hiding something from him, but he didn't ask his father for an explanation.

From then on, Sigmund suffered from night sweats and frightening dreams, and he became more and more depressed and in emotional pain.

*   *   *

On one of the Gentile holidays, Peter and Irena invited all their friends for a festive meal. Ziggy looked at the beautifully set table, piled high with delicacies, and his memory took him far, far away. In his mind's eye he saw many, many people sitting around a festively set table. He remembered only one thing more about that occasion: A boy joyfully stole something from his father, and not only was he not punished for this, but he was promised a reward — and only then did the boy return what he had stolen.

While Ziggy was in the middle of his reverie, he overheard Irena telling Peter about an event that had been celebrated in their neighborhood. She mentioned in German, "*Herr Falk hatte auch gekommen*," which means, "Mr. Falk also came." Ziggy shook himself free of his thoughts and exclaimed, "Yes! Yes! The stealing game is called *auch gekommen*!" (Ziggy had confused "*auch gekommen*" with "*afikomen*".)

"The stealing game?" asked Peter in surprise. "What is the stealing game?"

"You'll see," answered Ziggy. "I steal something from you, and you tell me to return it, but I say that I won't until you promise me a reward."

"All right," sighed Peter, "I give you permission to do it, just so you'll be in a good mood."

The meal began, and Peter soon regretted that he gave in to his son's whim. At that meal Ziggy's aptitude for sleight of hand was revealed for the first time, as one after another of the many guests discovered that some item of his or her jewelry had suddenly vanished.

Peter blushed with shame. He hadn't intended for the guests to also be victims of the stealing game, and he yelled, "Ziggy! I want you to give Mrs. Klopstock and Mr. Otzenklotz their watches and chains back immediately!"

But Ziggy darted about the room with strange gaiety and cried joyfully, "No! I won't return anything until you promise me a reward!"

Peter had to promise Ziggy nine separate presents. Only then did the boy calm down and return what he had "stolen."

A wearisome six months passed. It became clear to Peter and Irena that if they didn't do something about Sigmund's complicated problems, not only would he lose his mind, but they would go crazy, too.

"We have no choice," said Irena. "We will have to consult a psychologist — even though I'm afraid that a psychologist might bring back the boy's memory."

"And I say that we should return the boy to his parents," said Peter.

Irena sighed and said, "Even I would gladly do that, but it's too late. If we return the boy now, they'll put us behind bars for kidnapping."

So an appointment was made for Sigmund with Dr. Karl von Glick, an affable man and an excellent psychologist. After the boy was seated comfortably, the psychologist asked, "Well, my young friend, what is it that's bothering you?"

"I am searching for something that is hidden deep inside me," answered Sigmund, "but forgetfulness always drives that something away," he concluded awkwardly.

"Do you mean that you are trying to remember things from the past that you forgot when you were sick?"

"Yes, exactly so! The past bothers me terribly. Every

time I get ahold of something, boom! it slips away from my memory."

"Your father told me about how frightened you were when you went for a cruise on the Rhine. Did you almost drown once? Do you remember? Or perhaps you saw someone drown?"

Sigmund shook his head. "No, I was never even close to drowning. I've never been near the sea or a river. But... wait a minute... Yes, maybe I read about a donkey that almost drowned, or maybe even saw one."

"A donkey?" Dr. von Glick raised his eyebrows quizzically.

"Yes," answered Sigmund with confidence. "I saw a donkey that almost drowned, and... help! A bee!" He screamed suddenly when he saw a bee buzzing around the room.

Dr. von Glick quickly chased the bee out of the room and closed the window.

"Why were you so afraid of the bee?" he asked Sigmund.

"Doctor," said Sigmund with his voice shaking, "let me tell you that when a bee stings a person, he can drown!"

"Drown because of a bee sting?" asked Dr. von Glick, taking off his glasses and looking closely at Ziggy.

"Yes. Believe me, I'm telling you that's the way it is. That's it."

"We're you ever stung by a bee?"

Sigmund frowned. "No, but maybe that donkey was?" He paused, then finally said, "I don't remember."

*   *   *

After several sessions with Sigmund, Dr. von Glick asked the boy's parents to meet with him.

After they had been seated, the psychologist asked them if their son had ever come close to drowning, or had ever seen someone drown.

"No," answered Irena quickly.

"Actually, yes," said Peter, whereupon Irena looked at him with fury. "My wife didn't know about it," said Peter, hurrying to explain when he saw the amazed look on the psychologist's face. "It happened about a year before Ziggy got sick. We went for a walk along the river, and Ziggy slipped and fell into the water. I jumped in after him and pulled him out, but he was terrified because the current had already begun to carry him away."

Dr. von Glick made a mental note to think later about Mrs. Kranker's anger at her husband's mentioning the incident by the river. He wondered what the reason for her anger could be. Finally, after a moment's pause, he said, "If so, your son is still suffering from that incident, even though he is not aware of it. You must get him used to water. That is very important.

"But there is something more: Your son loves animals, but at the same time is afraid of them. For example, in his memory he is very much afraid of a certain donkey, but also pities the creature. And he also told me about a lion that killed a donkey so that it wouldn't bray." (Dear reader, as you surely know, Ziggy was half-remembering the story of Rabbi Akiva's donkey. You can find it in *Maseches Berachos* 60b.)

Dr. von Glick paused again before continuing. "I've

thought of two ideas that might help your son. First, take him to the children's zoo as frequently as you can. There, he'll get to play with and feed the animals in a safe and relaxed environment.

"Next, give him magic lessons. You say he's extraordinarily quick with his hands. Magic lessons will allow him to excel in something unusual. This will build his confidence — and he'll be involved in something that will take his mind off the past."

So, after all his troubles, Sigmund Kranker started becoming involved with both animals and magic. Later, he became an extraordinary escape artist. He had always felt an inexplicable need to run away, to be free…

During the day, Sigmund didn't suffer from his thoughts. Only at night did he continue to search for his past — without success. Sometimes, he dreamed about *them,* and that made him very happy. But who *they* were, Sigmund could never figure out.

9

The Painters

If you remember, dear reader, Yossi, Rabbi Aharon Bloch's son, came to Israel not just to visit his uncle, but to immerse himself in the sweet and pure Torah of Eretz Yisrael. As *Chazal* say, "*Ein Torah k'Toras Eretz Yisrael* — There is no Torah like the Torah of the Land of Israel." He therefore decided to check out several *yeshivos* in Yerushalayim. He hoped at least one would let him spend a few weeks learning there, even though he was only sixteen. He left on a Tuesday, intending to return to Haifa and his uncle on the following Sunday.

*   *   *

When Dr. Bloch returned home after taking his nephew to the bus station, he decided to learn a little before he had to go to the museum. But then there was a knock on the door, and immediately afterward the doorbell rang.

Bloch sighed and called out, "Who's there?"

"The painters," said a polite voice in heavily accented English from the other side of the door.

"The painters?" asked Bloch in English as he opened the door.

His astonishment was boundless. In the doorway stood a man dressed in overalls and carrying a canvas bag. Behind him stood three other men. Two were carrying pails and brushes, and the third, a big man, carried a ladder.

Before Dr. Bloch could open his mouth, the whole party strode confidently into the apartment. The man with the bag, evidently the boss, turned to Dr. Bloch and said, "May I speak English? I am very new in the country, and do not speak Hebrew."

Bloch thought, "Aha! That's why they look foreign. They must all be *olim chadashim*, new immigrants. I wonder where they're from." Aloud he said, "Certainly, but please forgive me. There must be a mistake. I didn't arrange for any painters, and I don't want to have the apartment painted."

"What are you talking about?" said the boss painter loudly, his face showing signs of anger. "You called the office this morning and insisted we come right away. You yelled and complained that you had been waiting two weeks for us, so we dropped all of our other work and came here. And now all of a sudden you say you never called us?"

In the meantime, the helpers had put down the pails, brushes, and ladder, and were leaning on the wall waiting for the argument to come to an end.

Dr. Bloch answered the painter politely but firmly. "My good man, I did not order any painting, and I ask you to please leave. You are interrupting my learning."

The painter took a cell phone out of his pocket and

punched the numbers angrily. After a brief pause he said, "Hello, Ralph, the man here says that he never arranged for us to paint… What? You want to talk to him? Okay." Turning to Bloch, he said, "You tell the manager that you don't want any painting. He doesn't believe me." As he held the phone out to Bloch he said, "He speaks English, too."

Bloch took the phone and said, "Hello. Let me say right away that I did not talk to you or to anybody about painting!"

A pleasant voice spoke through the cell phone. "One minute, wait one minute please. Yes. I was checking our records and I see that you are right. We made a mistake. Please excuse any inconvenience we have caused. But as long as we're talking, I have an important favor to ask you."

"What's that?"

"I ask you to please do exactly what my men say. Do not resist in any way, because your visitors are likely to shoot first and ask questions later," said the polite voice, to Dr. Bloch's astonishment. The phone made a loud chirping sound — and suddenly two of the painters were holding guns.

The cell phone was silent, and the "boss painter" said, "Do just what we tell you, and don't try any tricks."

"Who are you?" asked Bloch, trying to pull himself together.

The man ignored the question. "We're going to take you with us now for a few days. Put your wallet and your keys on the table there."

Dr. Bloch did as he was told.

"What's this?" asked the boss painter, taking a gray card

Suddenly, two of the painters were holding guns.

from Dr. Bloch's wallet. "You'd better tell us the truth, or you'll be very sorry."

Dr. Bloch's face turned white. His voice shook as he answered. "It's to get into the part of the museum that isn't open to the public. There are electronic locks. You can't get in without a magnetic card," answered Bloch, a hopeless look on his face.

"Are those all your keys?" the man asked again. "Don't you have keys to the cases where the valuable exhibits are displayed?"

"Not here. They're all at the museum."

"Good," said the boss painter, scooping up Bloch's keys and examining all the cards and papers in his wallet. "We're going to need all of these."

"You're talking nonsense. You can't use my identity card or driver's license or anything. They all have my picture," said Bloch, hoping that the painter would unintentionally say something about their plans.

"It turns out that there are people in the world who sort of look like you," said the painter, laughing.

"Good. He's beginning to talk," thought Dr. Bloch. He took a deep breath and said, "You're on a dangerous adventure, and it can't succeed. No matter how much a person may resemble me, he isn't me. I've been with the museum for ten years. Everyone knows me personally, from Dr. Shimon Karish, my assistant, to Avraham Snapir, the janitor."

The painter laughed with genuine humor. "It seems there's someone who resembles you a little more than you think. Did you every hear about doubles? Anyhow, thanks for giving us those names just now." The man turned to one of the men with a gun and told him in German to write down the name of Bloch's assistant, Shimon Karish, and the janitor, Avraham Snapir.

Dr. Bloch bit his lips like a person who has said something and is now sorry he said it, but thought, "Good. They fell for my trick." He had deliberately switched the names he had mentioned. In fact, his assistant was named Dr. Avraham Snapir, and the janitor, Shimon Karish.

"Yes, yes," said the boss painter, "sometimes it's not a good idea to talk too much. Now, please pay attention. I want to make it clear that we're not interested in you, and we don't intend to do you any harm. If you don't try any tricks, you'll be safely back home in a few days."

"Yes," growled Dr. Bloch, "after you've taken everything you want from the museum!"

"That's true," said the boss painter pleasantly, "but the important thing is that you will be fine as long as you do what we tell you. Now you're going to have to dress up a little." He handed Bloch a dirty and paint-stained pair of overalls, pointed in the direction of the bathroom, and said, "Change into these work clothes."

Bloch took the overalls and began walking toward the bathroom, but the boss suddenly call out, "Stop! Before you go in, we have to make sure that there's nothing there that…" He turned to one of the men and said in German, "Fritz, go in there and make sure there's no alarm button or cordless phone or anything else like that." Fritz went into the bathroom and came out a moment later shaking his head. "It's all right. There's nothing fishy in there."

When Dr. Bloch went into the room, he immediately took a pen out of his breast pocket. He wrote three phrases on the wall in tiny Hebrew letters: "Beware of twenty elephants"; "The doubled word at the end of *Vayeishev*"; and "The third saying of R' Meir." He thought for a moment about whether what he had done was like writing words of Torah in a bathroom, but decided that he had done nothing improper. Then he quickly changed into the painter's overalls, put the pen in his new pocket, and left the room.

"That was fast," observed the boss painter with satisfaction. One of the helpers folded Dr. Bloch's clothes and put them into the canvas bag. Meanwhile, the boss painter took theatrical makeup from the bag and applied it to Dr. Bloch's face. He then sprayed Bloch's hair to make it look gray. Within two minutes, Dr. Raphael Bloch was unrecognizable.

"We're leaving now," said the boss painter, and Dr. Bloch left too, carrying a pail and brush, with two painters in front of him and two behind. They got into a van that was waiting in front of the building and drove off.

*   *   *

"You know, Reuven, it's peculiar," said Mrs. Shorr, one of Dr. Bloch's neighbors, as she peered through the window that overlooked the entrance to the building where the Blochs lived.

"What's peculiar?" asked Mr. Shorr.

"Ten minutes ago four painters went into Dr. Bloch's house, and just now, five left."

"What's so peculiar about that?" said Mr. Shorr, disparaging his wife's comment. "It's simple. A painter was working alone in the house, and now four others came to get him."

"Impossible!" declared Mrs. Shorr. I saw Dr. Bloch arrive home twenty minutes ago, and he wouldn't have left a painter alone in the house."

"Oy," sighed Mr. Shorr, "What would become of the world if you didn't keep your eye on it all the time through the window?"

"You can make jokes all you want, but it bothers me," mumbled Mrs. Shorr, her eye still on the street below her building. "Why all of a sudden do four go in and five come out? What's the name of that book that we used to read to the children when they were little? Wait, wait… Yes, yes… *Mohammed Ali and the Fifty Thieves*."

"You mean" — Mr. Shorr couldn't keep from laughing, but managed to say through his laughter — *"Ali Baba and the Forty Thieves."*

"Yes, yes, that's what I mean. It's been so long since I thought about it. There was something in that book like this, forty men going in and thirty-nine coming out. Maybe it sounds silly, but it worries me. If I weren't so embarrassed, I'd call Dr. Bloch and ask him to explain it himself."

*　　*　　*

About an hour later, Sigmund Kranker appeared in front of Dr. Raphael Bloch's building, wearing Dr. Bloch's clothes and repeating to himself that from now on he is Raphael Bloch, Dr. Raphael Bloch.

"Now that's really strange!" exclaimed Mrs. Shorr from her perch by the window.

"What happened now?" asked Mr. Shorr.

"Dr. Bloch just got home."

"What's so strange about that?" asked Mr. Shorr, yawning.

"What's strange?!" cried his wife. "Just that Dr. Bloch came home already! You tell me how he can come home a second time."

"You know what? If you're going to play detective, I will, too. Right, you told me before that you saw five painters coming out? So one of them was Dr. Bloch, who wanted to try being a painter, but when he saw that it was hard work, he came home." Mr. Shorr laughed loudly at his own humor. "Believe me, someone could turn that into a story."

"Ha, ha, ha. You're always joking. I must say, it's very annoying." With that, the conversation came to an end, and Mrs. Shorr went back to surveying the street with great interest.

It is astonishing how often sharp-eyed people discount what they see with their own eyes.

10
Avraham and Shimon

T he next day — after carefully studying a map of Haifa — Sigmund drove to the Haifa Maritime Museum in Dr. Raphael Bloch's car. He turned into the small staff parking lot next to the building. The guard recognized "Dr. Bloch" from a distance, and opened the gate for him.

"Well," thought Sigmund, "the parking lot guard was the first test, and I passed it."

When he reached the door to the museum, he stopped to read the notice. It said, "Staff Entrance Only. No Admittance to Unauthorized Persons." He took out the gray plastic card with the magnetic strip that Big Ralph had given him along with the real Dr. Bloch's documents and keys, and put it into the reader on the wall. The door buzzed. Sigmund put on an expression of confidence, took a deep breath, pushed the door open, and strode briskly in. He hoped to find "his" office quickly and spend the day holed up in there. In the evening, when everyone went home, he would look for — and hopefully steal — the Red Pearl.

Mrs. Levy, the secretary, saw Sigmund as soon as he came in and rushed over.

"Good morning, Dr. Bloch. There are some letters and a lot of faxes for you, and Alon, the guide, has called in sick. All of the other guides are either not at home or unavailable today. What should I do?"

"What should you do?" said the new Dr. Bloch in his best American-accented Hebrew. "You'll just have to post a sign to inform visitors that there is no guide today, but that they are welcome to look at the exhibits by themselves."

"But Doctor, what about that busload of tourists from abroad? Yesterday you told us to be especially polite to them. They should be here any minute."

Sigmund was perplexed for a moment, but then to his relief remembered that he had an assistant, and that the assistant's name was Shimon. He turned to his secretary and said, "I'm especially busy right now with scientific matters and cannot think of other things. So for the next few days, please refer all administrative questions to Shimon, and follow his instructions."

Mrs. Levy was astonished, and her surprise and puzzlement showed plainly on her face. "Ask Shimon?" she said. "Does he understand enough?"

"Certainly. He knows at least as much as I do," answered Sigmund, and quickly went into the room with the nameplate "Director" on the door. He hoped no one would notice that he was able to unlock the door without the help of Dr. Bloch's keys. He made a mental note to figure out when he was alone which key opened which door. In the meantime, however, he was grateful for his training as an escape artist.

"Looks like the boss is so busy with his research that he doesn't even know what he's saying," thought Mrs. Levy. "He really is an 'absentminded professor'! Who ever heard of such a thing — to ask the janitor for advice! But what business is it of mine? I'm just the secretary. He said to ask Shimon? So I'll ask Shimon."

Shimon was busy polishing the floor of one of the corridors when Mrs. Levy approached him and asked, "Shimon, what should we do? There are no guides today, and that group" — she waved in the direction of a large group that was milling about the entrance — "is waiting for one."

"So why are you asking me?" asked Shimon. "Ask the director."

"The director himself told me to ask you."

"Me?" asked the janitor in astonishment.

"Yes, you! And tell me what to do already, because there's no guide."

Shimon thought for a moment and then asked, "What country are those people from?"

"Argentina," answered the secretary impatiently.

"Fine," said Shimon. "I can speak Spanish."

"So what?"

"So I'll be the guide myself," answered Shimon with air of importance. "After all, I must have heard the guides explain the exhibits hundreds of times. They always say the same thing. I could wake up from a sound sleep in the middle of a tour and still be able to finish giving the speech word for word."

Shimon walked over to the group of visitors and told them he was their guide. They gathered around him, and he took them from exhibit to exhibit, repeating the explanations he had heard so many times — but sometimes adding his own touch.

"Excuse me, what's this?" asked an elderly tourist pointing at a slender fish skeleton four feet long.

"This…is…the…" Shimon said slowly. He remembered something like "skamerdine," and struggled to remember the rest. Finally he decided what it must be and announced, "Ah! This is the skeleton of the longest sardine in the world."

"A sardine that long?" The visitors said in amazement and crowded around the exhibit case. Shimon, pleased as he could be, felt pride in his museum — and in his "sardine."

*   *   *

Meanwhile, Sigmund was sitting at Dr. Bloch's desk. He opened the drawers one at a time and memorized what was in each one. He also went through each key on Dr. Bloch's ring and figured out what it opened. Then he found another set of keys. "These must open the cases where the valuable exhibits are displayed," Sigmund thought to himself. "Panno mentioned that Dr. Bloch said they were here."

Unexpectedly, there was a sharp knock on the connecting door between the director's office and his assistant's office. Before Sigmund could say, "Come in," the door burst open and the assistant director, Dr. Avraham Snapir, rushed in. "Good morning, Raphael," he said. "Quick — do you have any rags in here?… Ah, here's one!" Dr. Snapir grabbed a rag

"This is the skeleton of the longest sardine in the world."

that was lying on a bookshelf in Dr. Bloch's office. He turned and rushed back through the door, saying over his shoulder. "I'm telling you, Raphael, I spill my tea every time. I have a real talent for it."

When the assistant director came rushing in, Sigmund didn't know who it was. But when the intruder picked up the rag, Sigmund thought — he was wrong, of course — that it was the janitor. But he wanted to make sure. He remembered that the real Dr. Bloch had let slip that the janitor's name was Avraham. So he called in a loud voice, "Avraham!"

Dr. Snapir appeared in the doorway and said, "Yes, Raphael. What is it?"

"Ah!" thought Sigmund. "So I was right. This is the janitor." Aloud he said, "My dear mister janitor, in the first place, one does not burst into the director's office that way. Also, you may not call me by my first name. Furthermore, I suggest that you not wear such nice clothes when you clean. Finally, I am very busy, and every interruption disturbs the progress of my work. Therefore, I ask you to please clean somewhere else. For instance, the floor near the entrance is quite dirty."

Dr. Snapir's eyes widened in astonishment and he exclaimed, "What's come over you, Raphael?" But then he burst out laughing and said, "Great! That's great, Raphael! At last, some signs of a sense of humor! I like that. It's healthier."

While Sigmund was wondering whether perhaps one didn't rebuke insolent janitors in Israel, an urgent knocking was heard and the door to the director's office was thrown open.

Mrs. Levy burst in and said, "It's impossible, Dr. Bloch, just impossible! We'll look like fools! Shimon is very polite, but he talks nonsense. Just now I saw him by the goldfish aquarium with the group, and he was telling them that we extract gold from the fish by a secret process. That's outrageous!"

Sigmund was silent for a moment, but then decided that as the director he couldn't let everyone say whatever they wanted — because then they might suspect that he wasn't Dr. Bloch. So he said to the secretary, "Please go back to your office at once. Dr. Karish knows his job better than you do." Then, turning to Dr. Snapir, he decided to take a different tack: "As for you, Avraham, I appreciate your friendliness, but right now I would like you to do me a favor. Take the rag and clean wherever you want, but not in this room."

Avraham Snapir stood with his mouth agape. But Mrs. Levy said, "Don't be alarmed, Avraham. The director is very busy with an important research project. He told me himself that he can't pay attention to administrative details." Then she turned to Dr. Bloch and said, "Perhaps in the meantime, until you have time for the museum's problems, you would be willing to have your assistant Dr. Avraham Snapir give me orders, and not 'Doctor' Shimon Karish the janitor? I'm sorry to interfere, but I thought that it would be better for you give authority to your assistant rather than to the janitor."

Sigmund's face turned white. He realized he had made a terrible mistake, and now he feared that the secretary and Dr. Snapir would begin to be suspicious of him. His mind worked furiously, and as it did his face became whiter and whiter.

It was actually his pallor that saved him. When Dr. Snapir saw the director's pale face, he was alarmed, and he said firmly, "Raphael, this can't go on. You're not taking care of yourself. It doesn't matter how important your research is, your health is more important. Look how pale and confused you are. You must have been up all night. Do you want me to drive you home?"

Sigmund sighed with relief. The color slowly came back to his face. In a weak voice he said to Dr. Snapir, "I don't need to go home. I just felt faint. And you're absolutely right, Shimon — excuse me, I meant Avraham. I didn't sleep a wink last night. I was concentrating on some tiny letters and trying to decipher them." He turned to Mrs. Levy and said, "Could you bring me a glass of water and two aspirins, please?"

After the secretary left, Dr. Snapir said firmly, "You're going home now. I'll call a cab if you'd rather I stay here. I don't think you can drive. And you're going to go to sleep immediately. I insist on that."

Sigmund had no choice. He had to give in and pretend that he was weak and sick. He got into the cab, accompanied by the worried looks of his assistant and the secretary, and rode home. He would have to postpone his plans to find and steal the Red Pearl until the next day.

11
The Robbery

Whon Sigmund got to the museum the next day (by cab, because his car was still parked there from the day before), he announced to everyone that he was feeling fine. He asked his assistant Dr. Snapir to handle the routine work so that he would be free for his own pursuits. He spent the day perusing the science journals Dr. Bloch got from various English-speaking countries. By five o'clock, he was waiting impatiently for everyone to leave, having told both Dr. Snapir and Mrs. Levy that he would be working late.

After everyone had finally gone home, Sigmund left his office and went through the entire building to make sure that he really was alone. After that he returned to the exhibition galleries. He systematically went through them looking for the Red Pearl. It wasn't on display.

Sigmund went back to his office and took the gray card for opening electronic locks as well as the keys to the closed exhibits from the desk drawer. Just as he was leaving, he noticed for the first time a framed photograph on the wall. It

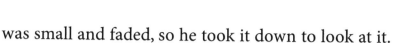

was small and faded, so he took it down to look at it.

It was a picture of three boys who looked so much alike that Sigmund was amazed. They were wearing warm winter clothes and standing by a snowman. Sigmund found the old picture very moving, though he couldn't say why. He looked at it closely for a long moment, then he sighed and put it in his briefcase.

He left the office again and went straight to a gray steel door he had noticed earlier marked "Closed Exhibits. No Admittance." He put the gray plastic card in the reader on the wall, and when he heard the lock buzz pulled the card out and pushed open the door.

Sigmund found himself in a large, dark room, filled with rows of glass cases of different sizes. Finding a switch on the wall, he flicked it on. Instantly, each case became illuminated by a narrow but bright beam of light. It was a breathtaking sight, like a dark field filled with fireflies. Not bothering to find the switch that turned on the main light, Sigmund went straight to a case that was near the center of the room. He stood in front of it and looked at the illuminated display. He felt as if he were hypnotized.

Behind the glass gleamed the Red Pearl in all its splendor. He was overawed, and stood looking at it for a long time. Then he looked at the lock on the case and saw that he could open it easily even without a key. But he saw a thin wire in the glass, which meant that the moment he opened the case in an unconventional way, an alarm would go off. Sigmund looked at the keys he was carrying, and tried to figure out which one would open the case housing the Red Pearl. Suddenly, a figure raised itself from the floor at the far end of the room, and a voice said, "Excellent, doctor! I've come at just the right time."

Sigmund spun around and saw a dark man with a bushy mustache and a hooked nose pointing a pistol at him. He recognized the man as someone who worked for the museum.

Sigmund was terrified. "What do you want?" he asked in a choked voice.

"What do you think I want?" the man began as he walked toward Sigmund. "Some old fish fossils? I'm obviously trying to steal that precious pearl, but you interrupted my work. I thought I would have to disable the alarm to get it, but you've just made it easier for me by coming yourself with the keys. The only problem, of course, is that I'll have to kill you after you open the case for me."

Sigmund broke out in a cold sweat when he realized what kind of danger he was in. His only hope was using his physical strength and the quick reflexes that he had honed from his years as an escape artist. "Well, well, well," he thought ironically, "I am about to perform the most important escape of my life."

By this time, the criminal was on the other side of the Red Pearl's case, facing Sigmund. Sigmund pretended to fiddle with the keys, trying to buy some time and collect his thoughts. The words *"Shema Yisrael"* inexplicably kept flitting in and out of his thoughts. Although he understood what the words meant, he couldn't understand why his mind kept saying "Listen, Israel," over and over again.

"Hurry up, Dr. Bloch," the thief urged nervously. "I haven't got all night."

Sigmund bent over the glass case as if to open it. The man was right next to him, breathing heavily with excitement. At that moment — and so fast that the man was taken completely by surprise — Sigmund jumped up, kicked his assailant in the knees, and punched him hard on the jaw. This knocked him out. Sigmund then took the gun out of the criminal's hand and used the butt of the weapon to break the glass encasing the Red Pearl.

At that instant, a deafening alarm was heard, and in the nearest police station a red light blinked. Sigmund quickly exchanged the Red Pearl with an imitation that he had been given, and which had been in his pocket. He then aimed the pistol at the thief lying on the floor, praying he wouldn't regain consciousness.

In a matter of minutes, three police vans arrived. When all sides of the building and all the entrances were covered, a squad of policemen forced their way in. A few minutes later, they came out with the handcuffed museum employee.

One of the policemen brought a chair and helped the trembling Sigmund sit down. He listened as Sigmund described the ordeal he had just gone through. "Dr. Bloch," he said, "I still can't believe it! How did you know how to save yourself from that dog?"

"Just let me go home," said Sigmund, still shaking. "I have to rest."

The next day, Friday, the newspapers reported in detail how Dr. Bloch of the Haifa Maritime Museum had disabled

Sigmund jumped up, kicked his assailant in the knees,
and punched him hard on the jaw.

an armed robber and thereby prevented the theft of the Red Pearl.

No one could have imagined that the unique pearl actually was stolen, and that it was in Sigmund's pocket.

*　　*　　*

In light of all the excitement, Ralph decided that Sigmund should keep the pearl until Monday. By then, the hullabaloo over the attempted robbery should have passed, and things should have gotten back to normal. Sigmund could then pass the pearl to one of the gang members at some place they would decide on.

12

What's Wrong with Uncle Rafi?

Yossi came back from Yerushalayim early Sunday afternoon. He hugged Sigmund with feeling and said, "Uncle Rafi, I'm so happy! What a miracle! *Baruch Hashem* that He saved you!"

Rabbi Aharon Bloch, Yossi's father, called a few hours later.

"My beloved Rafi," he said to Sigmund, "you should know that Hashem did a great and tremendous miracle for you. But I must tell you that you committed an *aveirah*."

Sigmund recognized the Hebrew word, but he didn't know what the rabbi was talking about. "A sin? Why?" he asked.

"Because life is immeasurably more important than money. Everyone is praising you for having the courage to attack an armed criminal. But what you did showed cowardice, not courage. You should have given up the pearl. According to Torah law, it was your obligation to turn off the alarm and let the thief take the pearl."

Sigmund was silent. "What can I say?" he thought. "This

Rabbi Aharon doesn't know that even if I had wanted to, I couldn't have turned off the alarm. And besides, the robber said he was going to kill me anyway."

"Therefore," continued Rabbi Bloch, "I have a *safek* whether you should say *birkas ha-gomel*, and I think you should ask a *posek*.

Sigmund was confused by these words. They meant nothing to him — not in English and not in Hebrew. So he said nothing, and Aharon Bloch explained the matter with the heated enthusiasm of a yeshiva student explaining a subtle point to his *chavrusa*, lapsing into Aramaic and Yiddish from time to time.

"You understand?" he asked. "*Leis mon d'paleig* (meaning, no one disagrees) that you really showed tremendous strength in knocking the guy out. That's *milsa pshita u'nehira* (something plain and clear). But *mei'iedach gisa* (on the other hand), we should be using our *kochos l'Oraysa* (our strength for the Torah). Be *me'ayein a bissel* (study a bit). Just open up *Beitzah b'kaf-hei* (*Maseches Beitzah*, on page twenty-five), and look at the Rashi on *daf beis* (the second side of the page). The *Yidden* (Jews) use their strength for *shteigin* (intense Torah study), not to put themselves in *sakanas nefashos* (danger)."

Sigmund was stunned by this hail of incomprehensible words. The only thing he understood was the sentence, "Open up an egg into coffee" (because he knew that *beitzah* means egg, and he mistakenly thought that Rabbi Aharon Bloch said "coffee," not "*kaf-hei*"). Therefore, he came to the conclusion that it is a Jewish custom to eat an egg mixed with coffee when one has been saved from danger. He wanted to bring this complicated conversation to an end as soon as possible, so he quickly said, "Rabbi Bloch... I'm sorry, I mean Raphael... I mean... I'm sorry, my dear brother Aharon, you're absolutely right. I'll have an egg in a cup of coffee right away, and I won't forget to add the rest."

Rabbi Bloch was alarmed by what his brother said. "Something's wrong with him," he thought. "It seems he hasn't gotten over the fright and shock of having a gun pointed at him — and now he's talking nonsense." He said aloud, "Raphael, the most important thing for you to do is rest, and you'll see that everything will be all right." He asked to speak to his son, and then said good-bye to his brother.

Sigmund sighed with relief and quickly handed the receiver to Yossi.

"Shalom, my beloved Yosef," said Rabbi Bloch. "I'm very eager to hear your impressions of the Yerushalayim *yeshivos*, but there is something more urgent. Did you notice how poor Uncle Rafi was talking? He's completely confused! First he called me 'Rabbi,' and then he said that he was going to eat an egg in coffee. Imagine that! This is Uncle Rafi, who is always warning me to keep away from coffee. Have you noticed other strange things in the way he acts?"

"Yes, Abba," Yossi whispered into the telephone. "First of all, he asked me where I had been for the past five days, as if he didn't remember that I went to Yerushalayim to look at *yeshivos*. Then, just a little while ago, he ate some cake and drank some water without making a *berachah* on either one!"

"What?!" said Rabbi Bloch in astonishment. "He must be suffering from serious psychological trauma because of everything that happened to him with that would-be thief. I'm flying to Israel immediately. I know there's a late-afternoon flight on El Al. Rafi's condition has to be taken seriously. People who are not given proper treatment after an experience like that can become dangerously ill.

"*B'ezras Hashem*, I'll be in Haifa tomorrow afternoon. Until I get there, keep your eye on him. Make sure that he doesn't do anything dangerous, like absentmindedly cross the street without paying attention to oncoming traffic. And if he faints or vomits, call an ambulance immediately."

"Yes, Abba," said Yossi, who already shared his father's anxiety. "I hope this passes quickly and Uncle Rafi recovers."

"Don't be upset with me for being so alarmed," said Rabbi Bloch to his son. "I hope it's nothing serious. But… but you know I've already lost one brother."

That very evening Rabbi Bloch boarded a flight for Israel.

*　　*　　*

Yossi didn't sleep at all that night. He felt that he was responsible for his uncle. "Poor Uncle Rafi," he thought, "to be face-to-face with an armed criminal and to have your life on the line — no one would be normal after an experience like that."

Sigmund Kranker also had trouble falling asleep. The next day he had to deliver the pearl to a member of the gang, and then check that the money promised him had actually been deposited in his account. After that, he had to rush to the airport and get on his flight.

Sigmund knew he should sleep, but something was bothering him. He knew that he wanted to think about something or do something, but couldn't remember what. He got up and began to pace back and forth in the room. Finally, he remembered what he wanted to do: He wanted to study the old photograph that he had taken from Dr. Bloch's office in the museum, and which was now in the inner pocket of his jacket along with various papers.

Sigmund sat down on the edge of the bed and gazed at the picture. It showed three boys, whose resemblance to each other was remarkable, standing by a snowman. The three resembled Yossi, too. Sigmund felt that his soul was in a tumult. He focused his thoughts, he frowned in concentration, but in vain. The cloud of forgetfulness overcame him as always.

From his own room, Yossi heard Uncle Rafi pacing the floor. He began to worry. He lay in bed trying to decide what to do, hoping that his uncle would go back to sleep. After what seemed like forever, the sound of his uncle's footsteps stopped, but instead of feeling relieved, Yossi felt more anxious. Finally, he got up and crossed the hall to Uncle Rafi's room, knocked on the door, and opened it a crack.

"Are you all right, Uncle Rafi?" he asked.

"Yes, absolutely. I'm just trying to remember something. But tell me, why aren't you sleeping?"

Yossi mumbled something about Haifa being muggy after the clear air of Yerushalayim. Then Sigmund said, "If you're awake anyway, maybe you can help me with something." He held out the framed photo to Yossi and said, "This picture reminds me of something that's important to me, but I can't put my finger on what. Do you recognize it?"

"Of course I do. You showed it to me last week. That's the three of you — Abba, you, and… but you know… Moishy."

"Moishy? Ah, yes… Moishy! Umm…" Sigmund didn't know who Moishy was, but he knew that to reveal that would arouse suspicion. On the other hand, it was important for him to know more about the picture, so he continued. "Yes, yes, of course… your father, me, and Moishy, but I've been trying unsuccessfully to remember what the occasion was for the picture. You surely know that in those days people didn't take a picture of every bit of foolishness the way they do nowadays."

Yossi was really alarmed by this and nearly started to cry, but he managed to control himself and say, "But Uncle Rafi, don't you remember what you yourself told me a week ago? The day I arrived you told me that this was the first picture my grandparents took with the new camera that they had just bought. And that they had three prints made, one for Abba, one for you, and the third for Moishy." He finished in an anxious voice, saying, "It scares me that you don't remember that." Sigmund mumbled something about how he was a little confused, and Yossi left the room.

Sigmund fell asleep half an hour later, while Yossi wandered around the house. He had been frightened by the conversation with his uncle, and all of a sudden felt very young. "Uncle Rafi has gotten so strange," he thought. "Can he be so confused just because of this business with the thief and the Red Pearl? Wait a minute… wait a minute! Wasn't he acting strange before that? Yes, he was!" Yossi remembered how his uncle had changed clothes after he left the main terminal building at the airport, and afterwards insisted that he hadn't been in the terminal, much less spoken with him. "Oy, poor Uncle Rafi! Who knows how long he's been this way! Maybe he's suffering from amnesia. Or maybe he has Alzheimer's. But that's an old people's disease!"

Yossi listened at the door of his uncle's room to make sure he was breathing. He so wanted his father to be with him during these difficult moments! He heard his uncle talking in his sleep and put his ear to the door so he could hear what his uncle was saying. He heard him say suddenly, "Here's the donkey, poor thing! I'll save you." Then his uncle said in a loud but frightened voice, "When are you going to chase that bee away? Ralph! Chase that bee away right now! You can have the pearl, just chase it away!"

His uncle's voice began to tremble as he said, "No! No! Wicked bee!" A horrifying scream escaped from his uncle's mouth, and then silence reigned. Uncle Rafi slept quietly again and his breathing was quiet and regular.

13

A Riddle in the Bathroom

Yossi could hold back the tears no longer. He stood and cried bitterly. "Uncle Rafi is suffering terribly," he thought. "He must be having a nervous breakdown, and I'm here all alone!" He went to the telephone and called home. His mother answered. "Imma," he sobbed, "I'm all alone, and Uncle Rafi is having a nervous breakdown… No, no, Imma, it has nothing to do with the foiled robbery. He was confused when I arrived in Israel. I'm afraid. Uncle Rafi is acting like a stranger…" His voice broke and he began to cry again, but he quickly got control of himself.

Yossi's mother listened to the rest of the story, and then tried to calm him down. "Soon it will be morning there," she said, "and, with Hashem's help, Abba will arrive at noon and take a taxi straight to Haifa. Don't worry so much. And… Yossi, you can call any time you want to."

Yossi, who had calmed down a little, said good-bye to his mother, hung up the phone, and went into the bathroom. He washed his face and cried, and once again washed and cried.

As he was drying his face, he noticed some tiny scribbling high up on the wall. Yossi bent his head toward the wall and strained his eyes. "Those are Hebrew letters," he thought. "It appears to be a riddle. It doesn't surprise me that Uncle Rafi made up a riddle, but it's strange that he wrote it on the bathroom wall, of all places."

Yossi quickly brought paper and a pencil and copied the writing (which had been written by Dr. Bloch at the time of the kidnapping). This is what it said:

להזהר מעשרים פילים — המלה הכפולה בסוף "וישב" — המשל השלישי של ר' מאיר

Beware of twenty elephants — The doubled word at the
end of *Vayeishev* — The third saying of R' Meir

It was three o'clock in the morning. Yossi was tired, but didn't want to fall asleep. He was glad to occupy himself with solving the puzzle of the strange riddle. First he took a *Chumash* and found the end of *Parashas Vayeishev*. In the fourth verse from the end, chapter 40, verse 20, of *Bereishis*, he found, "… and he raised the head of the chief butler and the head of the chief baker…" Yossi wondered if the riddle was referring to the word "head," which appeared twice in the verse. Or perhaps it referred to the word "three," which appeared twice in verse 18: "… the three baskets are three days…"?

He also wanted to know what the third saying of R' Meir was, but didn't know — although he thought it might be about a fox and a wolf. "And what in the world could be the connection between an elephant and the number twenty?" he wondered. He strained his mind trying to answer the question, "What is the connection between an elephant, a fox, a wolf, the number three, the number twenty, and a head?" Various ideas occurred to him, but he discarded them all.

"I'll have wait until morning and ask Uncle Rafi himself," he thought. "I hope that poor Uncle Rafi will even remember that he wrote the riddle."

At three-thirty in the morning, Yossi called home, where it was eight-thirty in the evening.

"Why aren't you asleep?" his worried mother asked.

"I don't want to go to sleep if I'm alone with Uncle Rafi and we don't know what's wrong with him," Yossi answered. "I'll sleep when Abba gets here."

"And how is he now?"

"He's sleeping quietly, and hasn't made any more frightening cries. I go to the door of his room every once in a while to make sure I can hear his breathing."

"Don't overdo it, Yosef," said his mother with concern. "You can certainly go to sleep. But if you'll feel better staying awake — then do whatever you need to feel safe and comfortable."

"Thank you, Imma," said Yossi, and continued. "I have a favor to ask. I've been trying unsuccessfully to solve a riddle. I have to know what the doubled word at the end of *Parashas Vayeishev* is. I tried 'head' and 'three,' but neither makes sense. And I also need to know what R' Meir's third saying is."

If Yossi's mother thought that her son was making a strange request, she didn't say so. Instead, she answered him, "I can tell you the answer to your second question. I actually taught it a few months ago. The third saying of R' Meir is, 'The righteous man is extricated from affliction, and an evil man will take his place.' The saying itself is from *Mishlei*, and R' Meir discusses it in *Maseches Sanhedrin*. Over there it says that R' Meir had three hundred parables using foxes, but we only know three of them. This is the third one.

"As for the doubled word at the end of *Parashas Vayeishev*, I'll try to figure it out. I'll call you back in a few minutes."

Yossi got up, when suddenly an idea came to him. "Just a minute," he thought. "Who said that this is a riddle? Since when do you write a riddle on the bathroom wall, and in such small letters, too? But if it isn't a riddle, what could it be? What's the meaning of that strange sentence?"

Yossi went back into the bathroom. This time he paid attention to the fact that the tiny letters had been written quite high on the wall. "It looks as if the person who wrote it didn't want others to discover what he had written. Perhaps it's a warning from Uncle Rafi. But who was he warning, and why?"

Yossi sat down again with the piece of paper on which he had copied the strange words and tried to fathom their meaning. "Twenty elephants, twenty elephants. Hmm. Maybe I need to look at this another way." He paused, thinking, praying for clarity. "Hey!" he thought, "maybe it doesn't mean the number twenty, but it's *Gematria*. The number twenty is the *Gematria* of the Hebrew letter *kaf*. If so, what's written is not 'twenty *pilim*' — elephants — but '*kaf-pilim*.'" He scribbled something on the paper: כ פילים. That's it!" Yossi cried. "Uncle Rafi meant כפילים, *kafilim*'!" Yossi knew that the word had something to do with כפול, *kaful*, double, but he couldn't remember exactly what it meant.

Then the telephone rang. It was his mother. "Yosef," she said, "first of all, the three sayings about foxes from R' Meir appear on page 39a in *Sanhedrin*. Second, I think the doubled word at the end of *Parashas Vayeishev* is in chapter 40, verse 15: '*Ki gunov gunavti* — For I was *surely* kidnapped from the land of the Hebrews.' The *Chumash* doubles the word for kidnapped in order to emphasize it."

"Thank you, Imma!" said Yossi. He felt his skin prickle with dread. He was about to hang up the telephone when he remembered that he had another question. "Imma, doesn't the Hebrew word *kafilim* also mean something about a double?"

"Ho ho, I see that this is a long riddle," his mother said. "The word does mean 'double.' The singular form, *kafil*, is a person who is like another in every way without being a relative."

"Oy!" said Yossi and fell silent.

"Hello! Hello!" said his mother in alarm. "Yosef, are you all right?"

"Yes, Imma, everything is okay," he said — but was really quite sure that nothing was okay. The writing on the bathroom wall had suddenly become an explicit warning. Yossi said good-bye to his mother, bent over the paper, and wrote, "Beware of twenty elephants — beware of doubles. The doubled word at the end of *Vayeishev* — 'For I was surely kidnapped.' The third saying of R' Meir — 'an evil man will take his place.'"

He wrote the solution: "Beware of doubles, because I was kidnapped and an evil man took my place."

"Could it be?" he thought. "Not only could it be, but it was written explicitly: Uncle Rafi was giving a warning that he had been kidnapped and a criminal had taken his place, someone who was his double — that is, completely identical to him.

"But what if all this is just a figment of my wild imagination?" Yossi continued in his thoughts. "Who said that this is the meaning of those strange words?

"On the other hand, it explains everything! It explains how I could meet two Uncle Rafis at the airport, and why Uncle Rafi suddenly doesn't know the first thing about *Yiddishkeit*, and why he didn't recognize the family picture — and, above all, the meaning of the strange warning in the bathroom.

"But if this isn't Uncle Rafi, then why did he risk his life to protect the Red Pearl?

"I have to find real proof! I have to know for sure whether the man sleeping across the hall is Uncle Rafi or a criminal pretending to be him. But how can I find out? Oh, Hashem, help me find an answer!"

Yossi closed his eyes and concentrated, and suddenly an idea came to him. Uncle Rafi had an old notebook with fingerprints, and Uncle Rafi's own were the first set in the notebook. He somehow needed to get the fingerprints of the man sleeping across the hall, and compare them to Uncle Rafi's in the notebook.

If the fingerprints were identical, then the man across the hall was indeed Uncle Rafi, and in need of medical attention. But if the fingerprints of the man with whom he was sharing this apartment were different from Uncle Rafi's, then the police should be called, not a doctor, to arrest the impersonating double and extract from him where the real Uncle Rafi was.

But how could he get fingerprints from the "uncle," from the man sharing this apartment with him?

Yossi thought and thought, and a plan began to form in his brain. First, he checked the cabinet where Uncle Rafi kept various things needed for household repairs, and was pleased to find a small bag of plaster for patching holes and nicks in the walls.

Then Yossi went into the kitchen, where he had noticed earlier that a baseboard tile had become detached from the wall. He took the tile and placed it on the kitchen table.

Dawn was breaking, and Yossi hurried to his bed in order to pretend to be asleep — before the unknown "uncle" woke up and found him too wide awake.

14

Traces on the Tile

Yossi lay drowsing, being careful not to fall into a deep sleep, until he heard the alarm clock ringing in his uncle's room. He looked at his watch. It was six-thirty. Sigmund got up, dressed, washed, and then went to the kitchen to make himself a cup of coffee. When Yossi heard this, he got up, stretched, and hurried to wash his hands. Then he went to the kitchen and greeted his uncle.

"Good morning, Uncle Rafi."

"Good morning, Yossi," Sigmund answered. "I see that you finally managed to fall asleep, but look how wrinkled your clothes are! You must have fallen asleep in them."

"It seems I did," Yossi answered and yawned. "If you're going to shul now, I'll go with you."

"Oh, no, no," chuckled Sigmund. "I just got back."

"Aha!" thought Yossi. "That's a lie if there ever was one. Either that or a false memory. After all, I heard Uncle R — I mean, this man — wake up, and I know he hasn't set foot outside the apartment yet this morning."

Yossi was still thinking about this when Sigmund said, "I'm going to be very late coming home this evening, so don't worry about me."

"Okay," said Yossi. "When will you be back? Five o'clock? Six?"

"I wish," answered Sigmund. "I have a meeting with a scientist from France this afternoon. He won't even get to the museum until five o'clock, and our meeting probably won't end before seven. And afterwards I have to take care of some pressing business. I won't be home before eleven." As he said this, Sigmund was thinking that at eleven o'clock that night he would actually be far, far away, safely back in Germany.

"Wow," said Yossi. "Until eleven o'clock? That is late. I can learn part of the day, but I thought I'd also like to make some small repairs in the house. For example, when I first got here, I noticed that one of the baseboard tiles in the kitchen had come loose. Last night I put it on the table here to remind myself to ask you if I can cement it back in."

"I'll be happy to have you do it. As far as I'm concerned, you can fix anything that needs fixing. Just don't make too big a mess." Sigmund was so relieved that Yossi didn't want to come with him to the museum that he would have let Yossi do almost anything.

While Sigmund was eating, Yossi mixed some patching plaster with water and spread it on both the baseboard and on the back of the tile. He made sure that he "carelessly" got some of the sticky mixture on the front of the tile as well. As soon as he had pressed the tile into place, he cried, "Oh, no! I almost forgot! It's near the end of *zeman Kerias Shema*.

Uncle Rafi, could you hold the tile in place for a few minutes while I say the *Shema*?"

"Of course," said Sigmund. He didn't know what Yossi was talking about, but he wanted to be amiable. He got down on his knees and held the tile in place while Yossi went out of the room for a short time.

"Thanks," said Yossi when he came back. He took over the job of holding the tile in place, but he was careful not to press in the center, where his uncle had touched it.

"I see that you're not the cleanest workman in the world," said Sigmund. "Both of my hands have plaster on them."

"I'm sorry, Uncle Rafi. But don't worry — I'll clean up whatever mess I make."

Sigmund went to wash his hands. Yossi looked at the tile and his heart filled with excitement and relief. His uncle's fingerprints were clearly visible in the plaster.

At nine o'clock Sigmund set out for the museum. As he said good-bye to Yossi, his eyes suddenly filled with tears. He was parting forever from this boy who reminded him of something in his own past that was far away and unknown. He sighed and left.

*   *   *

The first thing Yossi did when his uncle left was daven *Shacharis*. It was hard to keep his mind on his prayers, but he knew that no matter what, davening had to come first. How could he possibly merit help from Heaven if he wasn't fulfilling *ratzon Hashem*?

After Yossi finished davening, he opened the drawer

where the fingerprint notebook was kept. In a few moments he would finally know whether the man who had slept here last night was his Uncle Rafi or an impostor.

The notebook trembled in his hands as carried it into the kitchen. There were five small fingerprints in the first row. Above them were written in a childish hand, "My fingerprints — Raphael Bloch."

Yossi strained his tired eyes and carefully studied his Uncle Rafi's fingerprints. Then he got down on all fours and peered at the fresh fingerprints on the baseboard tile. Over and over again, he looked at the old notebook and then at the tile, trying to compare the prints. His aching head turned from the baseboard to the notebook, and from the notebook to the baseboard. His heart beat wildly. He became convinced beyond a doubt that the fingerprints on the wall were not the same as Uncle Rafi's.

"This is really unbelievable!" he thought. "Poor Uncle Rafi has been kidnapped and I'm living with a criminal impostor! I have to call the police!"

But then, without his knowing why, Yossi's eyes moved down to the second row in the notebook, to another five small fingerprints. Above these were written, "My brother — Moishy Bloch."

Yossi studied the fingerprints of the lost brother carefully, whereupon an impossible idea suddenly came to him. He raised his eyes and looked at the fingerprints on the tile. Chills ran up and down his spine. He cried out as if he had just been scalded. The fingerprints were identical to those of the lost Moishy!

Yossi looked at the fingerprints on the tile.

Yossi felt dizzy, and his head throbbed. As he got up, his dizziness increased, and the walls began to turn. He ran out of the kitchen and threw himself heavily onto the couch.

"Moishy is still alive," he murmured. His eyes slowly closed, and he fell into a deep sleep.

15

Willi Gets into Trouble

igmund arrived at the museum and went into his office. He was feeling nervous, and tried to calm himself. "Everything is under control," he thought. "All I have to do is get through the day, and then I'm on my way back home to Germany. I'll try not to talk to too many people at the museum so I won't make any blunders."

He looked at his watch. It was ten-thirty. According to the plan, in another half hour he had to leave the museum and meet one of the gang members to hand over the Red Pearl. Then he would return to the museum and wait. After Sigmund had delivered the pearl, Ralph was supposed to phone in a wire transfer of half a million dollars to the Swiss bank account that Sigmund had opened right before he left for Israel.

At noon he would call his bank to see if the money had been deposited. If it had been, he would leave the museum and go to the airport. He had reservations and a ticket for a flight to Europe at five o'clock in the afternoon. But if it turned out that Ralph had not wired the money — aha! In that case he would go to the police and tell them the whole story, including his part in it. He would not let Ralph cheat him.

Sigmund thought about how clever he had been to leave in his Cologne safe deposit box a letter describing the gang's plans in detail — and to mention this to Ralph. Were it not for that, Sigmund believed, Ralph would do whatever he had to do to get rid of him.

Then something occurred to him. "Are you really so smart after all? Who gave you the idea and the strength to overcome the robber? Wasn't it the Almighty God? And is He now pleased with the crime in which you are now actively involved?" Sigmund felt pangs of conscience for a moment, but he quickly brushed them aside.

*   *   *

At eleven o'clock Sigmund left the museum and set out along the seashore promenade, which passed directly below the museum. He walked slowly, occasionally looking around. Suddenly, he heard a voice call in English, "Charity! Give charity to poor Willi! If only I could be a magician!"

It was Willi, one of the gang members, sitting on a bench, and "If only I could be a magician" was the code that Sigmund and Ralph had agreed upon. Sigmund stopped. He took some small change out of his pocket, along with the pearl wrapped in aluminum foil, and dropped it all into the outstretched hand of the "poor beggar."

Willi shoved the foil-covered packet deep into his pocket. He stayed on the bench while Sigmund kept on walking.

Ten minutes later, Sigmund was back in his office at the museum, waiting impatiently for the time when he could call his bank.

*   *   *

Willi sat for a while longer. He then got up from the bench and walked slowly and carelessly, until he reached the parking lot where he had left the car that Panno had rented for him. He stopped by the car, took a ring of keys from his pocket, and unlocked the door.

Two policemen were standing some distance away. One of them noticed a man who looked like a beggar opening a car door. "Hey, Yoav," he said to his partner, pointing to Willi, "doesn't that look funny to you? I have a feeling that that character opens cars that don't belong to him."

Willi got into the car, started the motor, and roared off with the tires squealing. "After him, quick!" said Yoav. The two policemen jumped onto their motorcycles and drove off after Willi.

Willi drove very fast and was not far from the house that the gang had rented — and where the real Dr. Bloch was being kept prisoner — when he heard a siren and saw a police car in back of him. The cops signaled him to pull over to the side of the road and stop. Willi did, and one of the officers approached his car while the other radioed in a description of the car and its license number. The policeman by the car asked for Willi's driver's license as well as the car's registration, and when Willi replied in English that he didn't understand Hebrew, the policeman asked him again, in English.

From the registration papers, the policeman learned that the car was rented, and he asked Willi if he was the person who rented the car.

"Of course," he answered. "I mean, it was my friend who actually rented it, but there are three of us allowed to drive it."

"May I see the rental papers?" asked the policeman.

"I'm not sure that I have them — just a minute — yes, here they are!" said Willi politely, but he was wishing with all his might that the policemen would just leave him alone.

The policeman studied the rental agreement carefully and said, "It's in order, except it doesn't say that anyone other than the renter is allowed to drive the car. All it says is that someone named Panno Ricci rented the car, but your name is Wilhelm Hochstadt."

Willi was getting annoyed. "So what?" he said. "Panno is a friend of mine, and at the car rental place they told us that two additional people may drive it."

The policeman was also getting impatient. "Yitz, maybe you can explain it to him," he called to his partner.

The second officer walked over to the car and said, "Look, mister, it doesn't say here that you rented the car, and it also doesn't say that you are allowed to drive it. Because it doesn't, we're a little worried — and the chances are we're wrong — but we're afraid that maybe — maybe this is a stolen car."

"What a nerve!" said Willi angrily.

"I'm very sorry," said the first policeman, "but you are going to have to come with us to the police station. Then we'll see whether your friend Mr. Ricci or the rental company confirms what you say."

"So call from here!" yelled Willi. "How come I have to go with you to the station?"

"I'm sorry, sir, but those are the rules."

Willi's mind worked feverishly. "That's all I need," he thought, "to go to the police station. There they may search me and find what's wrapped in the aluminum foil. No, I have to make a break for it, come what may!"

Angrily, he said to the policemen, "What kind of police state is this… Hey, wait! It's a good thing I remembered. The form with the names of those who are allowed to drive the car is in the trunk. I'll show it to you."

Willi got out and walked toward the back of the car while the policemen waited by the door. But when he got to the trunk, instead of opening it Willi dashed off as fast as his legs could carry him.

The policemen were completely unprepared for this, and stood stock still for a moment. But then they recovered their wits and began to run after Willi, who had jumped over a wall and was sprinting through the yard of a house.

Willi was a good runner, but no matter how hard he ran, he could still hear the footfalls and heavy breathing of the police officers who were pounding along after him, not willing to give up the chase.

*　　*　　*

About an hour earlier, Rabbi Aharon Bloch had left Ben Gurion Airport. He immediately got into one of the waiting taxis and set out for Haifa. Now, he was standing by the stairs that led up to the building where his brother Raphael lived.

Willi dashed off as fast as his legs could carry him.

At that moment, after a wild run through backyards and over front lawns, Willi reached a street that he thought he recognized. He stopped to rest, but was on his way again before he caught his breath. As soon as he started running, he remembered why the street looked familiar: right in front of him was Dr. Bloch's apartment building.

He was trying to decide where he should run now when he saw two other policemen coming toward him. He turned around, but he saw the policemen who had arrested him. He had no choice: he took the stairs that led to Dr. Bloch's building. He was breathing hard, and he didn't know how he would get up the two flights of stairs to Bloch's apartment after running what seemed to him like a mile. He stopped to take a deep breath, and then — what a miracle! There, standing right in front of him, was Sigmund Kranker, dressed in a perfect Jewish rabbi's costume!

Willi had no idea why Kranker was dressed up, but at that moment, with the police hot on his heels, he couldn't have cared less. He took the foil-wrapped pearl out of his pocket and held it out to the man he thought was Kranker. "Take it back — quick! Get it to Ralph yourself — I'm in a mess!"

Before Rabbi Bloch could say a word, Willi shoved the small packet into his hand, dashed around the corner of the building, and dived head first into a gigantic flowerpot that was waiting to be filled with soil and have a tree planted in it.

Seconds later, four police officers came charging up the stairs. Two went into the yard, one on each side, and the other two pounded forward toward the building, passing Rabbi Bloch on the way.

Rabbi Bloch stared after the police officers bounding up the stairs inside the building. He wondered if his strange encounter with that man had anything to do with the policemen. But then suddenly the police came out of the building, ran down the stairs to the street, and raced up the block.

After collecting his wits, Rabbi Bloch put the little package in his pocket and hurried into the building and up the stairs. Before knocking on his brother's door, he carefully opened the package and, to his astonishment, found the Red Pearl.

He carefully rewrapped the pearl and put it in his pocket, and then knocked lightly on the door. When there was no answer, he knocked harder, and finally rang the bell for a long time.

Yossi, who had fallen asleep only three hours earlier after having been awake all night, finally woke up and opened the door.

"Abba!"

"Hello, my Yossi!"

They hugged each other, and then Yossi said, "Thank God, Uncle Rafi is okay."

"Really?" said his father. "*Baruch Hashem*! I'm so happy to hear that."

"I mean, he's okay medically, but…" Here, Yossi began to babble. "Uncle Rafi was kidnapped, and someone who looks very much like him is impersonating him. A real double. And I think it was all to steal the Red Pearl."

"What are you talking about?" demanded Rabbi Bloch, half annoyed and half mystified. "Where did you get such a crazy idea?"

"I'll explain right away, Abba, but first I have to tell you the rest of my news: This man, I mean the criminal who is Uncle Rafi's double, is a relative of ours. He is none other than your brother!"

"Again, what are you talking about? Are you saying that your Uncle Raphael is a criminal?" Rabbi Bloch was completely confused by now.

"No, I'm talking about Moishy! And I'm serious. Moishy is alive, and he is the person who took Uncle Rafi's place when Uncle Rafi was kidnapped."

Rabbi Bloch didn't answer. He just shook his head and finally said, "No!"

"Come over here, Abba, and sit down. I'll get you a drink of water and then I'll explain everything."

16

Ralph Tries Again

Finally, it was twelve o'clock. Sigmund picked up the phone. "In a minute I'll know what the story is at the bank," he thought. "Willi must have gotten to Ralph's apartment by eleven-thirty. Certainly half an hour is plenty of time for Ralph to call his bank and make a wire transfer to my bank in Switzerland."

Sigmund called his bank. It didn't take long for him to find out that not a cent had been deposited in his account. Angry, he considered calling Ralph immediately, but after a moment's thought decided to wait fifteen minutes before doing anything. "Maybe Ralph couldn't get through to his bank right away," he thought. "Or maybe Willi was delayed in some way." He watched the clock tensely — waiting for a quarter after twelve.

*   *   *

The policemen searched every corner of the garden for Willi, but didn't think of looking in the huge flowerpot that was standing there. After Willi heard them leave, he waited a few minutes before climbing out of his hiding place and running quickly to the gang's apartment. There, he burst in like a storm wind. "It's about time you got here!" said Ralph angrily, his patience gone. "You almost gave us all an ulcer. Now give me the pearl!"

"Kranker will be here in a few minutes and give you the pearl himself," said Willi, breathing hard.

"Kranker? What are you talking about?" yelled Ralph. "He told me explicitly that he was going to stay at the museum until he needed to leave for the airport."

"I know, boss," said Willi, "but I guess he had some kind of a problem. Let me tell you what happened. I'm driving along, and all of a sudden I'm stopped by the police..." Willi described the chase to Ralph and continued, "...and then, just when I'm sure it's all over, I look up and see Kranker right in front of Bloch's building."

"What nonsense!" cried Ralph impatiently. "Kranker is at the museum!"

"Boss, I'm telling you the simple truth. It was Kranker. He was dressed up like a very dignified Jewish rabbi. But then I heard the cops pounding after me. What could I do? I gave him the pearl and told him to bring it to you himself."

"You gave the pearl to a rabbi who looked like Kranker?" asked Ralph slowly in a threatening tone.

"No, not to someone who *looked like* Kranker. To Kranker, who for some reason was dressed as a rabbi. I had no choice. The cops were about to grab me. I had to get rid of it."

Ralph got up, livid with fury, and slapped Willi's face so hard he knocked him down.

"Idiot! Worthless fool! You gave the pearl to Rabbi Bloch and not to Sigmund Kranker! I'm sure of it. He obviously came here after his son. If I don't get that pearl back, I won't envy you."

At that very moment the phone rang. Ralph was so angry that he nearly ripped out the receiver in picking it up.

"Ralph" — it was Sigmund — "I see you decided to try to make a fool of me. I handed over the pearl at eleven o'clock, as we agreed. It is now twelve-twenty, and nothing has been deposited in my account. Now listen, Ralph: If within fifteen minutes you don't call your bank and wire into my Swiss account the miserable few dollars you are throwing me, I will call the police here and turn us all in. I won't mind sitting in jail as long as I know that you'll be there."

"Instead of talking like a fool, why don't you calm down and help us solve a problem?" shouted Ralph. "Just two minutes ago the idiot you gave the pearl to walked in and told us that he doesn't have it. He gave it to Rabbi Bloch, Dr. Bloch's brother."

Sigmund felt his nerves giving way. He yelled, "I'm not interested in the stupid things your helpers do. I did what I was supposed to do, and you have to pay me — immediately!"

"Stop shouting!" Ralph shouted. "If you want to act like a donkey, go right ahead and turn us all in to the police. Within two days, I'll be out — I have connections and friends — but you'll sit in jail for a good few years along with Panno, Willi, and a few other bright fellows. On the other hand, if you want to act like someone with a brain, help us get the pearl back from Rabbi Bloch. Instead of half a million, I'll pay you a full million."

Sigmund thought for a minute and then said, "I'll do it, but only if half of it is in my account within a quarter of an hour."

"Agreed," said Ralph. "I'll see that it's done."

Sigmund calmed down a little. "What exactly do you want me to do?" he asked.

"It's very simple," answered Ralph. "Go back to Bloch's apartment and act as if nothing has happened. Rabbi Bloch will undoubtedly tell you the whole story and give you the pearl, thinking that you are Dr. Bloch — that is, his brother."

"Fine. I'll call you back in fifteen minutes."

When the time was up, Sigmund called his bank in Switzerland. Ralph had kept his word; half a million dollars had indeed been deposited into his account. He called Ralph and said, "Okay; in half an hour I'll pretend to finish up here and go home — that is, to Dr. Bloch's home — to exchange a few words with Rabbi Bloch."

*   *   *

"It's all your imagination," interrupted Rabbi Bloch while Yossi was explaining about the riddle, the double, and all the rest. "You can't accuse someone of being involved in a crime on the strength of some scribbling on the bathroom wall."

"Please Abba, just let me finish. I have clear proof. Look at those fingerprints in the plaster. Can you make them out?"

"Yes."

"Okay. Now I'll bring the notebook with Uncle Rafi's fingerprint collection. He has Moishy's fingerprints, too. If you see that Moishy's fingerprints in the notebook are the same as the ones on the tile, will you believe that Moishy took Uncle Rafi's place here?"

"I will have no choice but to believe, but it just doesn't make sense."

Yossi hurried to get the notebook with the fingerprints.

*   *   *

While Yossi and his father were talking, Ralph was issuing hurried orders to his men. "I'll leave soon and wait near Dr. Bloch's house, to get the pearl from Kranker. In the meantime, you will arrange everything for our departure. We will leave on the five o'clock flight, as planned."

"And what about our 'guest'?" asked one of the men, pointing to the room where Raphael Bloch was being held prisoner.

"We'll leave him to our brilliant friend," answered Ralph, turning to Willi — whose cheek was still red and smarting from the ferocious slap Ralph had given him. "Listen, Willi," he addressed him, "you will guard the doctor until four this afternoon. Then you will inject him with this hypodermic" — he held up a syringe — "so he'll sleep until tomorrow morning. Then you will take a cab to the airport, and get yourself on the next available flight to Europe."

"Yes, boss," said Willi.

"And don't let him go — even if you get it into your head that his name is Kranker, and even if suddenly he's dressed like a priest," said Ralph, while all of the gang members except Willi laughed uproariously. "Do you understand?"

"Yes, boss," said Willi, his rage boiling inside him.

"And one more thing," said Ralph. "You messed up so badly that I have no choice but to tell you that for the next three months you will work without pay."

Willi's face turned white, and he stared at Ralph in disbelief. Ralph continued in a voice that was cold and cruel, "And I hope for the sake of your health that we succeed in getting back the pearl you lost."

Willi kept quiet. He was afraid, humiliated, and furious — all at the same time.

Everyone left on his assignment, and when the door slammed shut, Willi was left alone with his burning cheek and his raging thoughts.

17

Dr. Bloch Persuades Willi

The prisoner — who was none other than the real Dr. Raphael Bloch — sat in his room and listened to the tumult on the other side of the door. He heard the insults that were heaped on Willi and all the talk about the pearl. After everyone left and the door was slammed for the last time, he called to Willi through the locked door of his room.

"What do you want?" snarled Willi.

"I heard your friends calling you sometimes 'Willi' and sometimes 'Hochstadt.' Is that your family name?"

"Yes. What's it to you?"

"Are you Jewish?"

"Yes. So what if I am?"

"I was wondering if you were related to Itzaleh Hochstadt, the famous cantor from Germany who was killed in Dachau."

Willi laughed bitterly and said, "Itzaleh Hochstadt was my father's uncle. He's the one who arranged for my father to be hidden by a Gentile family during the war."

"Do you also have some singing talent?"

Willi answered by singing Kol Nidre in a voice that was both strong and sweet, and filled with feeling. When he finished, Dr. Bloch applauded from the other side of the locked door. "That was wonderful," he said. "You really are a cantor! How did you know this prayer?"

"My father used to sing it at home. He told us children that he sang it constantly to himself the whole time he lived with the Gentile family. He said it kept him from forgetting he was Jewish."

The imprisoned doctor suddenly changed the subject. "What you did with the pearl wasn't very smart," he said.

"What could I have done?" Willi said with a sigh. "The police would have caught me with the pearl."

"In your place, I would have swallowed it, for example."

"I never thought of that," admitted Willi. "But even so, Ralph didn't have to treat me so terribly on account of a mistake."

To Willi's great surprise, Dr. Bloch said, "I understand why he was so angry that you lost the Red Pearl. But you possess a different pearl, and you are throwing it away."

Willi didn't understand this. "What are you talking about?" he asked.

"I'm talking about your singing talent. I know that a gangster can make a lot of money, but I am sure that as the cantor of a big synagogue in America you could earn a decent living, without being humiliated and getting your face slapped. And besides, at the same time you would be doing a mitzvah."

"A what?" Willi asked.

"A mitzvah," Dr. Bloch repeated. "A good deed. You would be helping the Jewish People — *your* people."

Willi didn't answer. Finally Dr. Bloch said, "Willi, listen to me!"

"I'm listening," he said, but actually he was remembering the old photograph his father had of Uncle Itzaleh Hochstadt. He imagined himself wearing the beautiful white *kittel*, with a high white yarmulke on his head, chanting before hundreds of people — with Ralph and the rest of the gang as his choir.

"For me, every minute is precious right now, Willi," said Dr. Bloch. "My double is already on his way, but if I leave immediately I might get there first. If I do, I will be able to recover the priceless Red Pearl that was entrusted to me."

"Yeah, and that's why I'm guarding you, so you won't leave," replied Willi.

"Listen to me, Willi," implored Dr. Bloch. "You have a choice. You can stay with your miserable gang, living on stolen money and having your boss humiliate and beat you, or you can help me get out of here. If you decide to help me, I'll help you get started as a cantor. Or, if you don't want that, I'll arrange for you to work in the museum. I'll also see to it that you get a small apartment rent-free. And don't forget the most important thing of all, Willi: Even if Ralph manages to get that pearl away from my brother, I have a feeling that your life will still be in danger."

Willi's heart skipped a beat. His life as a gangster passed before his eyes in a flash. He felt his burning cheek, his fear of

Ralph, and his desire to spoil his boss's plans. Would it really be possible to live differently? he wondered. He was sure that Dr. Bloch would keep his promises, so at least he would have work and a place to live.

"Please decide fast, Willi," said Dr. Bloch, pressing him. "I must get to that pearl before Ralph does."

Willi didn't answer. Instead, he opened the door to the room, unlocked Dr. Bloch's handcuffs, and held out his hand to the released prisoner.

Dr. Bloch shook Willi's hand with feeling. Then he wrote an address on a scrap of paper, handed it to Willi, and said, "Get in a cab and go to this address — fast. You can hide there until we're sure that you are in no danger from Ralph. I'll be in touch with you as soon as I can."

"Thank you, doctor," said Willi with emotion.

"Everything will be okay as far as the apartment and job I promised you," said Dr. Bloch as he rushed into the bathroom and washed off the theatrical makeup that the "painters" had put on his face as a disguise.

"I know you will keep all of your promises," said Willi, his eyes bright with tears.

"So long!" said Dr. Bloch, and disappeared out the door. As soon as he was gone, Willi remembered that Kranker was on his way to Bloch's house. He ran to the telephone to call Rabbi Bloch and warn him.

*   *   *

Yossi grabbed the notebook containing his Uncle Rafi's fingerprint collection. He brought it to his father and, pointing to one of the fingerprints, said, "See, Abba, here in the second row…"

The telephone rang, and Rabbi Bloch picked up the receiver. "Hello… Yes, this is Rabbi Bloch speaking," he said.

"Listen carefully, Rabbi," said the voice on the other end. "This is a friend. Right now, your brother Dr. Bloch is on his way to his apartment, where you are. But another man is also on his way there. I mean the double, who looks exactly like Dr. Bloch. I'm calling to warn you not to give the pearl to either one until you are absolutely sure who is the doctor and who is the double — the crook."

The blood drained from Rabbi Bloch's face. "Yes, I will do that," he said. "And I thank you from the bottom of my heart."

He put down the receiver and turned to his son. "You were right about the double."

"And the double is the missing Moishy!" added Yossi with feeling. "Look here, in the notebook…"

At that moment they heard quick footsteps and then a key being turned — and the front door swung open.

18
Uncle Rafi — Twice

A man strode into the apartment. "What a wonderful surprise! My beloved brother Aharon!" he exclaimed.

Until the telephone conversation with the anonymous "friend" half a minute earlier, Rabbi Bloch would not have doubted for an instant that the man who had just walked in was his brother Raphael, and he would have rushed forward to embrace him. But now he backed away warily and said, "Raphael, please don't come any closer. I have to make sure…"

He didn't have a chance to finish when they heard someone running up the stairs, and then another Uncle Rafi burst through the open door, panting and puffing. His face was dirty and he was wearing paint-stained overalls. "Aharon, I hope that you haven't given the pearl to this thieving impostor!"

"Stop!" cried Rabbi Bloch. "Both of you keep away from me. Don't come another step closer. No one is going to get the pearl until I know who's who and what's happening."

"Both of you keep away from me. Don't come another step closer."

"Excellent," said one of the Rafis. "Call the police. The best thing is for the police to get involved and find out the truth."

The other Rafi followed suit: "Absolutely. The best thing is to call the police."

Rabbi Bloch said, "Indeed, I shall call the police." He approached the telephone and said to the two Rafis that stood facing him, "The first one who takes a step forward will prove by his action that he is not the real Dr. Bloch."

He was lifting the receiver when Yossi cried out, "Abba, don't do it! Don't call the police! Do you want Moishy to go to prison?" He turned to the two Rafis and continued excitedly, "You, the double, the impostor, whoever you think you are, whatever you call yourself — I will tell you who you really are. Your real name is Moishy Bloch, and you are one of triplets. The other two are Dr. Bloch and my father, Rabbi Bloch."

Rabbi Bloch put down the telephone. He certainly didn't want his brother Moishy to get involved with the police. One of the Rafis looked with wonderment at his double and said, "Moishy? My double is Moishy? That's just impossible!" while the second Rafi said "Moishy? That's just impossible!"

Rabbi Bloch was still thinking about what to do when they heard someone say, "This is taking way too long!"

They all turned toward the doorway. There stood Ralph, with a pistol in his hand, and next to him stood one of his thugs — also holding a gun. Ralph kicked the apartment door closed with his foot. The four other people in the apartment backed away and stood close together.

"Rabbi Bloch, give the pearl to this man," he ordered, nodding toward the thug — while not for a second taking his eyes off the four people standing opposite him. "And as for the riddle of who is the real Dr. Bloch, I will give you the answer: The man in the painter's overalls is the real Raphael Bloch. Ha, ha, ha!"

Sigmund, who was dressed stylishly, strode victoriously to the doorway and stood next to Ralph. "Well, Rabbi Bloch," he said mockingly, "hand over the pearl as you were told. Don't forget, it was you yourself who told me that life is more valuable than any wealth. You do remember saying that, don't you?"

Rabbi Bloch sighed. He reached into his pocket, and his face turned as white as paper.

"I can't find the pearl! My pocket is empty!"

"Enough jokes!" cried Ralph angrily. He waved his gun threateningly.

"He's telling the truth," interjected Sigmund. "I have the pearl. You've forgotten that I'm a sleight of hand artist. When we all backed away from you, I took advantage of the confusion to take the pearl out of the Rabbi's pocket without anyone noticing." He took the pearl out of his pocket with a flourish and showed it to Ralph and his cohort.

"Sigmund, give it to me already!" said Ralph impatiently.

"First call your bank and give them the order to transfer the full amount you owe me to my bank in Switzerland. As soon as it is in my account, I'll hand over the pearl."

Ralph sighed and turned to his assistant. "Rudi, cover them with your gun while I make the call." He took out a cell phone and called his bank to give the order. While he was talking on the phone, Yossi turned to Sigmund and pleaded, "Please, Uncle Moishy, stop pretending. You're not Sigmund. You're Moishy Bloch. You're the third person in the picture you showed me last night."

Sigmund's face suddenly showed emotion, and Yossi continued as persuasively as he could. "Don't you remember that you almost drowned? Don't you remember Smith's donkey, and the bee that stung you? Please, please remember!" he pleaded.

Sigmund turned pale and trembled for a second, but the signs of emotion disappeared and his calm expression returned. "I have to leave now," he said to Yossi, "but I have your uncle's telephone number. If the truth is as you say, I'll get in touch with him."

Ralph nodded to Rudi, who took handcuffs and ropes out of his bag and proceeded to tie up hand and foot the rabbi, his son, and his brother. While Rudi was tying him, Yossi yelled, "Sigmund, look in the fingerprint notebook! There is clear proof there that you are Moishy Bloch!"

After all three had been bound so well that they could hardly move a muscle, Rudi gagged them with big handkerchiefs.

Sigmund looked at them with compassion, and wave of pity passed over him. He turned and hurried out of the apartment with Ralph and Rudi.

The three got into Ralph's car and drove off. Sigmund called his bank in Switzerland on his cell phone and this time, after a brief conversation, an expression of satisfaction came over his face. He took the Red Pearl out of his pocket and handed it to Ralph. Ralph looked at it with glittering eyes. "Finally! At last I've got it! And I already have a buyer, ha, ha!"

Two hours later, Ralph and four of his henchmen — along with Sigmund — were about to board the airplane that would take them back to Europe. Ralph suddenly realized that the real Dr. Bloch wasn't supposed to have been at his own apartment. In all of his excitement over the Red Pearl, he had completely forgotten about this detail.

"Aha!" he said. "Now I understand how the doctor escaped from his little prison — plain treachery. Willi decided to leave us and help the doctor. I'll deal with him when the time comes, but first I want to sell the pearl for a good price."

Six hours later Sigmund Kranker was home, and the next day he rejoined the circus and resumed his performances.

Only two weeks remained before the pearl would dissolve and disappear.

19

A Phone Call from Dr. Litmus

The three prisoners tried to free themselves, but they couldn't. They began to feel anxious because they had no idea how long it might be until someone came to untie them. Fortunately for them, about eleven o'clock that night, Willi decided to leave the apartment where he was hiding and go to Dr. Bloch's house. He knocked on the door lightly and then rang the bell, but he didn't hear anything from inside. He rang again and listened more closely. He thought he heard a sound like someone clearing his throat. Then he heard the sound again, plus something that sounded like the tapping of heels on the floor.

Even though it was very late, Willi ran to one of the neighbors and rang the bell. When the door opened, he apologized profusely and explained that he was worried about Dr. Bloch. "I'm afraid something has happened to him," he said. "He was supposed to be at home. When I ring the bell no one answers, but I hear sounds from inside."

The neighbor suggested that Willi call the police, but

Willi said he thought it would be better if the two of them broke open the door. "I take responsibility for anything that happens," he concluded.

Willi and the neighbor were trying to force open Dr. Bloch's door when a man from the floor above came down the stairs. He was wearing a robe over his pajamas and looked confused and a little afraid. When he reached them he said, "What's going on?" After the other neighbor explained the situation, he offered to help as well.

The three pushed on the door with all their might, but their efforts were in vain.

Finally, Willi asked the neighbors if they had any tools: a hammer, a chisel, maybe a small crowbar. The one from upstairs said he did, and ran to bring them. Willi tried to hide the fact that he was adept at opening locked doors with just a few simple tools, but very soon the door swung open.

Willi and the neighbors rushed in and freed the Bloch prisoners. When the neighbors had gone, the three sat down with Willi and everyone told the others his side of the story. Yossi showed his uncle the fingerprints on the baseboard tile. "There can be no doubt," said Dr. Bloch with feeling. "Our brother Moishy was here but slipped away to we know not where."

"So then what can we do to bring Uncle Moishy back to us?" asked Yossi impatiently.

Rabbi Bloch said, "I think the most important thing is to be quiet — I mean, not to reveal that Uncle Rafi was kidnapped and that a double impersonated him. If the police find out, they'll look for someone who resembles Uncle Rafi, and poor Moishy will end up in jail — something none of us wants. All we can do is find out quietly where someone who looks exactly like me and Raphael lives."

"You don't have to look too hard," said Willi, and he told them that Moishy, also known as Sigmund Kranker, was the well-known circus magician Gazlano the Great. "But you have a big problem," he continued. "This magician, that is, Moishy, doesn't know that he's a relative of yours. He believes he's the son of Peter and Irena Kranker, and a Catholic."

"That's right," confirmed Yossi, and he told his father and uncle how terrible it was last night when Sigmund asked him who the three children in the photograph were, and when he cried out in his sleep.

"Do you happen to remember what Moishy yelled in his sleep?" asked Rabbi Bloch.

"I remember it well," answered Yossi. "He said, 'Poor donkey, I'll save you,' and then begged someone to chase away a bee. The last thing he said was, 'No! Wicked bee!' and then he let out a terrifying scream."

The memory of that bitter day with Smith's donkey and the bee came back to Raphael and Aharon. They exchanged a meaningful look and sighed.

"That's actually a good sign — that he dreams about what happened to him," said Dr. Bloch. "It means that deep in his memory his past still exists, but in some confused way."

"And we know how to reach him," said Rabbi Bloch. "I propose that we write him a letter and tell him what happened to him when he was a boy. Maybe we should send pictures, too, and hope that he remembers."

The very next day, the brothers mailed their letter to Sigmund — Moishy — and waited impatiently for an answer.

Meanwhile, Rabbi Bloch and Yossi filled Dr. Bloch in on what had happened while he was being held prisoner by Ralph and his gang. He was astonished to hear that one of the museum's employees had actually tried to steal the Red Pearl.

The two brothers then went to a Rav to ask if they had to report the kidnapping. They explained that they were worried that Moishy — and Willi — might end up in jail as a result. Since Dr. Bloch hadn't been harmed in any way, he didn't want to risk putting two Jews behind bars.

The Rav ruled that if Dr. Bloch had no desire to press charges against his kidnappers, then he only had to report the theft of the Red Pearl. And because Willi's life might be in danger, Dr. Bloch wouldn't have to reveal any information about Ralph and his gang.

Dr. Bloch and his brother went from the Rav's house to the museum, where Dr. Bloch examined the "Red Pearl" — and found it to be merely a red marble. From there, the brothers went to the police. Dr. Bloch reported that when he went to examine the pearl that afternoon, he found that it was gone… and in its place was a marble made of red porcelain.

"The truth is," he said to his brother after coming home from the police station, "I'm almost glad that the pearl was stolen. On account of that we finally found Moishy, and we brought Willi back to an honest life. The only thing that troubles me is that the pearl wasn't mine, and in a few months the mysterious millionaire who loaned the pearl to the museum will ask me to return it."

Somehow, word got out that the Red Pearl had been stolen, and the next day the theft was reported in newspapers all over the world. That evening, Dr. Bloch got a long-distance telephone call.

"Hello, doctor," said the caller. "I read in the newspaper about the theft of the Red Pearl. I want to tell you that nothing of value was stolen. As far as I know, there is no such thing as a red pearl, and never has been. The stone you had wasn't a pearl at all."

"Who is this speaking?" asked Dr. Bloch.

"Does the name Ph. Litmus mean anything to you?"

"Of course!" cried Dr. Bloch. "One of the world's leading chemists! To what do I owe the honor of your call?"

Litmus laughed sadly. "At least there's one person in the world who respects me," he said bitterly. "I will repeat what I told you: The stone that was stolen from you was a fake. I cooked it up in my own kitchen, from materials that are found in every chemistry laboratory in the world. As I said, as far as I know, there are no red pearls and never have been."

"With all due respect, sir, why should I believe you?"

Litmus chuckled and said, "Because it was I who sent it to you. If I tell you exactly what day and hour you got the pearl, and describe the messenger correctly, will you believe me?"

"Yes, I will," answered Dr. Bloch.

"So. The messenger gave you the pearl at precisely two-thirty in the afternoon, seventy-three days ago. He told you he was representing a very wealthy man who wished to re-main anonymous. He was wearing a red leather jacket and carrying a dark blue briefcase."

Dr. Bloch thought for a moment. "Yes, it's just as you say."

"So, since seventy-seven days have passed since I made the pearl, it will melt and decompose in another thirteen, or at the most fourteen days, since I made it to last exactly three months."

"Very interesting," mused Dr. Bloch. "In other words, you really managed to fool us all."

"Indeed I did," Litmus said pleasantly. "But please," the chemist continued in a more serious tone, "I beg you not to repeat a word of what I said. I only told you so that you wouldn't be anxious about the pearl."

Dr. Bloch thought for a moment. "Okay," he agreed. "I won't say anything without your permission."

"Thank you," said Litmus gratefully, "and I sincerely apol-ogize for any distress I caused you. I know that your life was in danger because of the pearl, when that museum employee tried to steal it. I must admit that I had looked forward to making a fool of you and the entire scientific community. But when I saw just how high the stakes really were, I had a change of heart. I would never have forgiven myself if you had been hurt or...worse."

"Don't feel bad, Dr. Litmus," said Bloch. "Thanks to all your 'cooking,' I found my long-lost brother. By the way, didn't you once develop something that improves the mem-ory?"

"I did," confirmed Litmus.

"It may be that I will need your services," said Bloch.

"I will be happy to help, to make up for the trouble I caused you," replied Litmus. "I feel terrible about my foolishness. It was my pride that made me do something desperate."

"It's okay, Dr. Litmus. I understand. We'll talk again soon, I hope," said Bloch. "Thank you for relieving my anxiety about the pearl." The two men hung up.

Two days later, Sigmund Kranker got a small package from the two brothers. In it was a letter.

20

The Letter

Again and again Sigmund read the letter from Aharon and Raphael Bloch:

To Moishy, our beloved brother, whom we will never forget, full of mischief, who made sure our days were never dull — dear Moishy, for whose sake we begged our father many times with tears in our eyes not to give you the spanking you really deserved — Moishy, who dragged us into all kinds of dangerous adventures and in the end succumbed to the danger that he put himself into.

First of all, we want to tell you that you don't have to go into hiding or be afraid of the police. We have no intention of reporting you, even though if we did we might get the pearl back. You are dearer to us than all the pearls in the world.

Beloved Moishy, we heard from a friend that you are a professional magician and that you are certain that you are a Catholic. We want to tell you the truth about yourself, in the hope that you will remember.

Moishy, you are a Jew.

The three of us were born in the United States. We are enclosing the address of the Department of Vital Statistics in the town where we were born. You can write to them and get a copy of the relevant birth records and see for yourself that we are right. We have enclosed a photograph of the three of us taken when we were a month old, plus all of our full names and our birth date.

The summer when we were ten years old, we were in the mountains. One day, the donkey that belonged to our neighbor Mr. Smith got lost. You looked for it and found it on top of a certain hill at the bank of a river. We went with you to see the lost donkey. The mud on top of the hill was slippery, and every step was dangerous, but you were holding on to a big rock. Then, you were stung by a bee and loosened your grip on the rock. You lost your footing on the slippery mud and slipped and tumbled down the hill and fell over a cliff into the river and disappeared. How we cried! How long our parents searched for you — but nothing was ever found but your yarmulke — your skullcap. We are sending it, too. Perhaps it will help you to remember.

Whoever found you raised you as his own child, as a Catholic. But we want you to know the truth.

We have all the pictures of you from infancy until the day you disappeared. We imagine that you have no pictures from your childhood. Did you ever wonder why your parents — we mean the people who raised you, who you thought were your parents — didn't have any pictures of you until you were ten years old? The reason is that they are not your real parents. Maybe they saved your life, but they stole you from us. Please, Moishy, remember your past. Please come back.

If our beloved parents were alive, no doubt meeting them would return you to yourself. But they have been in Heaven for a number of years, and they look down on you and pray that you will return to the bosom of your family and your holy nation.

Moishy, in this package we have sent you many pictures and various items from your childhood. We also enclose a photocopy of your brother Raphael's fingerprint notebook, in which your fingerprints appear.

We hope that your memory will be awakened, but even if you don't remember, please ask yourself the following questions. We hope they will prove to you that you are Moshe Bloch and not Sigmund Kranker.

1. Your fingerprints appear in Dr. Raphael Bloch's notebook (from when he was a child). What are they doing there?

2. What is the explanation for the astonishing resemblance between you, Dr. Bloch, Rabbi Bloch — and even Rabbi Bloch's son Yossi?

3. Why (as you will see) do the birth records say that triplets were born to the Bloch family? We suggest you ask your "parents" where you were born, and you will see that your name does not appear in any German birth records. Why?

4. Why are we not informing the police about your part in the theft of the Red Pearl?

If you think about these things logically, you can come to only one conclusion: You are the lost son of the Bloch family. You are our brother! Our dear, dear brother Moishy!

We will be happy to talk to you whenever you want — maybe that way we will succeed in awakening your memory.

Joyful at having found you, and sorrowful at your distance,
Your brothers,
Areleh and Raphael

Sigmund folded the letter, but then immediately unfolded it and read it again.

He felt that between the lines of the letter loving hands were outstretched to him, as if to say, "Come back to us."

Sigmund did not see how he could accept the bizarre idea that he was a Jew and that Peter and Irena were not his father and mother. But he knew that if the Blochs were right — and he was the child that was stung by a bee and nearly drowned — he would understand why to this very day he was terrified of drowning and why every bee he saw threw him into a panic.

He decided to look into the matter seriously. The next time he went to visit his aged father, he would ask him some questions and then go to the municipal office in charge of birth and death records, to see if they had a record of his birth. If they didn't, then he'd take the brothers' unbelievable story more seriously.

Poor Moishy, a wicked man made it impossible for you to discover the truth. Who will open your eyes? Who will return your lost memory?

21

An Erroneous Conclusion

Two years before these events, Peter Kranker's wife Irena died.

As long as Irena was alive, Peter didn't even dare to think about the possibility of revealing the truth of Sigmund's past to him, because he was afraid of her anger — and also because he didn't want his wife to be accused of kidnapping.

After his wife died, Peter decided to tell Sigmund the truth at last, but every time he had a chance to do it, he couldn't get the words out. He just didn't have the courage to tell Sigmund, who loved him, that he was not his father — that he was really nothing more than a kidnapper.

The same thing happened now, when Sigmund visited his father, determined to find out the truth about his past.

He greeted Peter and said, "How are you, father? You look well."

Peter looked at his son and said, "It only looks that way. The truth is, I am a sick old man whose time has passed. Soon enough I will follow your mother."

"Don't talk that way, father!" cried Sigmund. He noticed that his father was holding a popular science magazine, and in order to change the subject, he asked, "What's new in the world of science?"

"As a matter of fact, I just finished reading something interesting," answered Peter. "I don't know if it will interest you, because you're not a science buff, but I read that a very rare gem that was discovered only two months ago has disappeared under mysterious circumstances, presumably stolen. It's called the Red Pearl."

"As it happens, I also heard about that," said Sigmund. "Does the article give any theories about how the pearl was stolen?"

"No. The director of the Israeli museum from which it was stolen, a Dr. Bloch by name, says only that when he went to check it one day, he discovered that it had been switched for a simple red marble."

"Does the article report that there were attempts to keep Dr. Bloch away from the museum in order to steal the pearl?"

"No. But why would you ask such a question?" asked Peter.

"No reason," answered Sigmund aloud, but he thought to himself, "So, Bloch kept his promise not to tell the police about me. I wonder why he did it, if not because I am his brother."

There was a pause. "You know, Sigmund," said Peter, clearing his throat, "we had neighbors named Bloch once."

"Really?" said Sigmund excitedly. "And were they relatives of Dr. Bloch from the museum in Israel?"

"That I don't know," answered Peter, and continued, "but I want to talk to you about something else. There is something that has been bothering me for a long time, and I've been wanting to talk to you about it. I am talking about… about…about…" But he couldn't continue. He felt as if the words were stuck in his throat, and once again he couldn't speak his mind.

"Does it have to do with me?" asked Sigmund, agitated. His heart began to race.

"N…no," stammered Peter. "I mean, yes…when…I mean…"

"What is it, father?" asked Sigmund expectantly.

Peter was silent for a while and finally, reluctantly blurted out, "Once, I borrowed quite a large sum of money from the Bloch family and… I'm ashamed to say I never returned it. I would like you to find the family, so I can return the money… Ah, but you really don't have to do that. I can do it myself."

It was clear to Sigmund that Peter was trying to evade his question, and he cried, "Father!"

"What do you want?" Peter asked, closed once again in his armor of silence.

"You have always been so good to me. You were always there for me when I was troubled. I want to know the truth. Am I a Jew, a son of the Blochs who were your neighbors, or am I your son?" Sigmund himself didn't know where he found the strength to ask such a question.

Peter turned pale. He didn't answer. He felt that he would never have the courage to tell his "son" the truth.

"Father, why don't you answer me?!" cried Sigmund, his heart aching.

"Because I'm upset and angry," answered Peter. "What has gotten into your head? Who could imagine that in my old age my son would question his identity and think that he wasn't really my son? Go to the Bureau of Vital Statistics here in the city and get a copy of your birth certificate." Peter knew what Sigmund would find there. He knew that Father Pancreas had managed to have Sigmund's birth records falsified right after he and his wife moved to Cologne, because among the papers that Father Pancreas had given him was a birth certificate saying that Sigmund Kranker was born in Cologne, Germany, in 1951.

"Father, please forgive me," Sigmund said contritely when he saw his father trembling.

"You don't have to ask forgiveness," said Peter, trembling like a leaf because of the powerful feelings of guilt that filled him.

"I hurt you, father," said Sigmund sorrowfully.

"Forget it. It's not your fault. You always suffered from nightmares, and this is just another one of them. Maybe it's our fault, for not getting you the kind of treatment you needed."

Sigmund left his father after apologizing again, and hurried to the Bureau of Vital Statistics. He filled out a form requesting a copy of his birth certificate and waited in line for a few minutes. When it was his turn, the clerk glanced at the form and asked for identification. Sigmund showed him his driver's license. "That will be ten marks, please," said the clerk. Sigmund handed over the money, and the clerk stamped the form and said, "The certificate will be mailed to you within a week."

"But this is urgent," said Sigmund. "I can't wait a week."

"I'm sorry sir, but we have procedures, and that's how long it takes."

Sigmund pleaded with the clerk. While he was talking, he slipped a fifty-mark note under the form so that just its edge was showing. The clerk didn't even notice. It was an easy trick for Gazlano the Great to do. Then Sigmund turned as if to go. The clerk looked down to pick up the form and saw the money. "One moment sir," he quickly called after him. "Perhaps if I speak to my supervisor..." Sigmund waited impatiently until the clerk returned with a copy of his birth certificate.

*   *   *

Sigmund was devastated. "I was suspicious for no reason, and I hurt my father because of the Bloch brothers' false accusation," he thought angrily.

Sigmund thought a lot about what the Bloch brothers had said. Yet his birth certificate showed in black and white that a Sigmund Kranker had been born in Cologne, Germany, in 1951. One simple, logical thought never occurred to him: If with a small bribe he could get his birth certificate without waiting a week, then with a big enough bribe, might it be possible to put a false birth certificate into the files? But he didn't think of that, so he wrote a letter to Dr. Raphael Bloch in Israel:

Dear Dr. Bloch,

First of all, I must apologize to you for your having been kept a prisoner for a week on account of me. On the other hand, you owe me thanks for having discovered — at risk to my own life — that one of your employees was a dangerous thief.

Next, my profound apologies for having taken the pearl. It is no longer in my possession.

I cannot thank you enough for keeping silent about my part in the theft of the pearl.

Finally, and most important: I got a copy of my birth certificate from the Bureau of Vital Statistics in Cologne, Germany. You are mistaken — I am not your brother. My name is Sigmund Kranker, not Moshe Bloch. I was born in Cologne, Germany, in 1951, not in 1950 as you and your twin brother were.

With thanks,
Your double (and not your brother),
Sigmund Kranker

*   *   *

When Yossi read the letter, he nearly cried. He pleaded with his uncle to let him visit Sigmund. "I will convince him that he is Moishy, not Sigmund," he said.

"Listen," Dr. Bloch said to his nephew. "Perhaps you were mistaken about the fingerprints after all. Everything we wrote to Kranker was supposition anyway. I guess we all got carried away with the possibility that he really was Moishy. Oy," Dr. Bloch sighed, "I still miss him so much."

There was a long silence. Then Dr. Bloch continued. The

only thing we can do now is to have *kavanah* when we say *Hashiveinu* that Hashem should return your Uncle Moishy also."

And what about Sigmund? Every evening he would study the photographs and the remnants of Moishy's childhood that he had been sent. He knew there was something that he himself didn't know. A sigh came forth from his aching heart, the sigh of someone caught in a whirlpool of emotion.

22

Pancreas Returns

When Big Ralph said that he already had a customer for the Red Pearl, it wasn't an idle boast. Even before he and his henchmen left for Israel, he had looked actively for a buyer — and found one: a wealthy and respected man.

Now, he was hurrying to the buyer's house. And who was the buyer? A man named Mr. Leopold Pancreas.

Mister Pancreas? Does the last name sound familiar, dear readers?

It should. Mr. Leopold Pancreas and the priest Father Pancreas, the man who helped the Krankers kidnap Moishy thirty-three years before — and who falsified birth records in both Germany and the United States to conceal the kidnapping — are one and the same person. Thirty-three years ago, he was supposedly just an ordinary priest who worked very hard at converting Jews, God forbid.

Well, the truth is that all those years ago, "Father" Pancreas was merely a two-bit criminal and nothing more. Leopold Pancreas was born in Germany in 1930. He spent the best

146

years of his childhood being indoctrinated in Jew-hating by the Hitler Youth — a pernicious, dangerous organization that trained German youngsters in the Nazi way.

By the end of World War II in 1945, the adolescent Pancreas had seen his whole world literally fall apart: The Axis powers had been defeated. He was poor and homeless. And he was totally alone, as his parents had been killed in an Allied air raid. By then, Leopold was not only a Jew-hater but an angry, hardened youth as well. The chaos in Germany was fertile ground for young Leopold to turn his hand to petty crime. He became a black marketer, selling contraband at gigantically inflated prices to the highest bidder.

Leopold made his way to Aachen, Germany. The Americans were stationed there as part of the Allied Forces' program to rebuild Germany after the war. And they always had money for chocolate and cigarettes — two of the most popular items for sale on the black market. Leopold was clever enough to display a charming personality, and quickly made friends with the Americans. In this way, he slowly learned English.

By the early 1950s, Leopold was tired of his "career" — although he had amassed quite a tidy sum of money. And besides, the German economy was already functioning well enough without black market goods. He wrote to one of his old American "friends" who was already back in the States, and persuaded him to sponsor his immigration application. Leopold told his friend that he had studied for the priesthood, and wanted to start a new life in America doing "holy" work. With his black market connections, it was a simple matter for Leopold to obtain a fake document from a non-existent Catholic seminary certifying that he was a recently ordained priest.

From there it was just a hop, skip, and a jump to America, the land of opportunity. Leopold figured that he could "set up shop" in a small town. He found the perfect venue in the Catskill Mountains in upstate New York. He had enough money to build a small church — and enough charm to acquire a small congregation of unsuspecting town residents. It was a wonderful cover for his more "important" activities, which were laundering money for the mob, obtaining forged papers for criminals on the lam, and arranging for stolen goods to make their way to Germany. He soon became a wealthy man.

By 1975, Leopold Pancreas had had enough of small-town American life and decided to return to his native land. With his underworld connections, he was able to resume his criminal activities in Germany. No longer did he have to pretend he was a priest, living the ascetic life. Now he could live as ostentatiously as he liked. He bought himself a huge home in the toniest neighborhood of Cologne and furnished it with the best that his money could buy. He also had the latest model BMW, as well as a Porsche for a little variety. The money kept coming in, and before he knew it, he was worth millions.

But of course, people like this can never have enough. Without simple good morals and ethics — and without the fear of Heaven — they spend their lives trying to acquire more, better, the best. For the next twenty years, Pancreas went from big house to bigger house, from fancy car to fancier car, and from local crime to international crime. So when Mr. Leopold Pancreas's old buddy Big Ralph approached him and offered to sell him the Red Pearl — which Big Ralph himself did not have yet — he jumped at the offer. And now, finally, Ralph and the pearl were on the way. Pancreas paced the floor impatiently, waiting for Big Ralph to arrive.

Dear reader, exactly ninety-one days had passed since Dr. Ph. Litmus had cooked up the Red Pearl in the kitchen of his house in Brussels, Belgium.

*   *   *

As Big Ralph walked up the stairs of Pancreas's imposing home, he found the signs of wealth so conspicuous that he decided to raise the price of the pearl. He and Pancreas had agreed on five million dollars, but looking around, he thought that this was too small a sum for someone so wealthy — and besides, obtaining the pearl had cost him extra, as he had to double Kranker's fee. He debated whether to ask for seven or eight million, but when he got inside and saw how luxurious everything was, he decided without hesitation on a round ten million.

Pancreas welcomed Ralph warmly, and the two of them went into the wealthy criminal's study.

"So?" asked Pancreas.

"What 'so'? Here's the goods," said Ralph. He took the Red Pearl out of his pocket, held it up so that Pancreas could see it, and immediately put it back in his pocket. "You have the money?" he asked.

"Well, yes. It was hard, but somehow I managed to get the five million for you."

"Hard?" Ralph laughed and continued, "Excuse me, but doesn't a man of your, uh, high social status, read the newspapers?"

"What do the newspapers have to do with it?" asked Pancreas.

"Didn't you hear that the key man in the operation was in danger — that he was nearly shot by an armed intruder? And there's something else you may not know. After we stole the pearl from the museum it slipped out of our hands. That Jew Bloch's brother got ahold of it and we could get it back only by outright robbery."

"What does all this mean?" asked Pancreas, knowing only too well what it meant.

"What does it all mean? you ask. A bonus for danger, and another bonus for the second robbery. I really should ask for fifteen million, but I'll give you a break and ask for only ten," said Ralph without blinking an eye.

"What? You low-down scoundrel! We agreed on five million, and you simply double the price. That's highway robbery!"

"Are you suggesting that I am now committing a third robbery in connection with the Red Pearl? That may raise the price some more."

"You are being ridiculous."

"True, my good friend," said Ralph, rising to his feet. "Maybe I will offer the Red Pearl to Mario. He'll pay me four times as much. He'll probably put it in a solid gold setting,

"I'll give you a break and ask for only ten million."

where it will decorate his large hand. Then he'll parade it all over Cologne for everyone to see and admire." Ralph laughed loudly and turned toward the door.

This was too much for Pancreas. "Hey, wait!" he cried.

"What should I wait for?" asked Ralph.

"Seven million and the deal is done," said the former fake priest.

"Ten million and not a penny less."

"Eight-and-a-half!"

Ralph opened the door.

"Sit down!" shouted Pancreas. "Sit down, you crook!" He left the room for a few minutes and came back carrying a valise. He put it down on the desk. "There is eight million inside, and here are two million more," said Pancreas as he put two large sacks down next to the valise. "Now give me the pearl."

Ralph handed the Red Pearl to Pancreas, who gasped in awe and excitement. Ralph smiled with satisfaction, but he was sorry that he hadn't asked for more. As he got up to go, he declared with a smirk, "It was a pleasure doing business with you." Pancreas ignored him, and Ralph left the room.

* * *

As soon as Ralph had gone, Pancreas telephoned his jeweler and "requested" him to come to his house later that afternoon. But a request from Leopold Pancreas was really an order — if you valued your health and livelihood. The jeweler said he'd be there in two hours.

The time left for the pearl was running out.

23

Pancreas Gets Burned

Exactly two hours later, Lucretius Colitis stepped into the lavish reception hall of the Pancreas residence. Having been the criminal's personal jeweler for over a decade, Colitis was used to frequent summonses to the mansion. Whenever he was bored, Pancreas would buy another jewel for his collection of rare and expensive gems. Therefore, Colitis had come well-stocked with all sorts of precious stones, hoping to make a lucrative transaction.

After exchanging greetings, Pancreas thanked Colitis for coming on time. "Actually, Mario asked me to swing by this afternoon as well," the jeweler said. "I'll be going to his house after we're through here."

"Excellent!" Pancreas thought to himself. "Colitis will tell Mario all about the Red Pearl. Boy, will he be disappointed that Big Ralph didn't offer it to him first — ha, ha, ha!"

The two men adjourned to the study and got down to business. "My dear Lucretius, you have undoubtedly heard of the Red Pearl, have you not?" inquired Pancreas.

"Of course! That rare gem that was discovered only a couple of months ago and then stolen. Do you know something about it?"

Pancreas chuckled. "As a matter of fact, I know quite a lot about it. In fact, you might say that I am intimately acquainted with the Red Pearl." And with a flourish, Pancreas whipped the stone out of his pocket.

"Wh...what...how did you get that?" cried Colitis, as he tried to get a better look at the gleaming red gem. For some reason, it was a much brighter red than Pancreas remembered it being.

"A group of worthy friends of mine — including a Jew whom I converted when he was a child — rescued the pearl from the Jews. I purchased it from them for the modest sum of ten million dollars. And now," Pancreas smiled, "I would like you to design for me a most appropriate setting. I want a ring that will show off the Red Pearl in all its glory, one that will be the envy of all my friends."

The jeweler was speechless for a couple more seconds. Then he said hoarsely, "May I, uh, examine the gem, please?"

Pancreas handed over the pearl to Colitis, who proceeded to examine it with his jeweler's monocle. "Astounding," he breathed. "A genuine red pearl." The jeweler silently gave it back to Pancreas, who held it up to the light with satisfaction and happiness. Suddenly he screamed. The pearl had begun to melt in his hand, and the chemicals released by its disintegration burned his fingers horribly. In vain, the frightened criminal tried to throw the pearl away, but it stuck to his

Suddenly Pancreas screamed. The pearl had begun to melt in his hand, and the chemicals burned his fingers horribly.

fingers like wet clay. As he shook his hand, red drops from the melting pearl flew up and burned his face while others dripped on his suit jacket and burned holes in it.

"Help! Help!" shouted Pancreas. His servant Heinz burst into the room. "Water! Quickly!" Pancreas groaned. "And bandages and something for burns and my doctor!"

The servant rushed out. He returned a moment later to say that Pancreas's personal physician was on his way. At that point, the jeweler got up and made his way to the door and out of the mansion.

"Aii!" Pancreas screamed in rage. "That rogue wanted to kill me!"

"Or at least," he thought to himself, "to injure me and making me a laughingstock. I'll never be able to look Colitis in the face again. He's probably on his way to Mario to tell him what happened. How will I ever hold my head up in this town again?"

The doctor came in and immediately gave Pancreas an injection. Then he applied a cream to Pancreas's burned hand and cheek. As soon as he felt a little better, his anger returned. It was clear to him that Big Ralph had tricked him. Not only had he swindled him out of ten million dollars and given him a bogus pearl, he thought, but to top it off he had brought disgrace down on him. No, he wouldn't take this lying down! He would either break every bone in Ralph's body, or he would inform on Ralph and his gang of rogues — even if he incriminated himself as well.

The second idea actually sounded very good to Pancreas. After all, it would be easy to cook up some story about how he had no idea that he was buying stolen goods. And he could always cover his bases by striking a deal with the police: information for them, immunity for him.

"Yes," thought Pancreas, "bringing Ralph down would be much better than merely breaking his bones." He smiled to himself and swallowed a painkiller.

24

Pancreas the Good Citizen

Thomas von Sauerbraten, chief of the Cologne police department, sat with his deputy Konrad Apfel. It was a slow Tuesday afternoon, and the two were bored.

"How about a game of cards, Konrad?" asked von Sauerbraten.

"Why not?" his deputy yawned, and got up to get a deck.

The two men were immersed in Go Fish when the phone rang.

"Von Sauerbraten here," said the chief. "Hmm…and he insists on seeing me now?" The chief looked at his deputy, who shrugged his shoulders and collected the cards. "Okay, send him in."

"What was that all about?" inquired Apfel as he put the cards away.

"None other than Leopold Pancreas himself wants to see me," his boss replied.

"Pancreas? What could he possibly want? He's a pretty

shady character. We never could put our finger on exactly what he does — or how he made all those millions."

"Well, we'll soon find out what he's here for," answered von Sauerbraten.

There was a knock at the door. "Come in," shouted the chief, and Pancreas entered the office.

"Mr. Leopold Pancreas, to what do we owe the pleasure of your company?" said von Sauerbraten as his visitor sat in an empty chair.

"As a loyal and law-abiding citizen, I feel it is my duty to apprise you of certain information which may be of great importance to you."

Apfel sniggered when Pancreas said "law-abiding," but von Sauerbraten threw him a look that said, "Keep quiet."

"Yes, Mr. Pancreas," the chief prompted, "please go on."

Pancreas was silent for a moment, as if trying to choose the right words. "Have you heard of the Red Pearl?" he finally asked.

"Of course," answered the chief of police. "It was stolen not long ago. I understand the trail that might lead to it is completely cold."

"Indeed," sighed Pancreas. "Well, a few days ago a man who introduced himself as a dealer in precious stones came to my house and offered to sell me a red pearl identical in every respect to the one that was stolen. I immediately suspected that the man was the thief himself — or someone connected to the thief — and that he was really offering me the stolen pearl. I questioned him at length, and he managed to convince me that this was a different red pearl. I bought it from him for an incredible price — ten million dollars."

Gasps of astonishment escaped from the two policemen.

"But I'm no fool," Pancreas continued. "I know something of gems. I examined the pearl very carefully. I had no doubt that this was a genuine red pearl. I thought, 'Why can't there be a second red pearl?'"

"I admit," continued Pancreas sanctimoniously, "I let my desire for that beautiful gem override my suspicions. I know now that I should have called the police. But just as I was considering what to do, a thought crossed my mind: Even if this is the stolen pearl, it's better for me to buy it and hand it over to the authorities. Otherwise, who knows? The thief could escape, or sell the pearl to another less scrupulous individual. Then, the owners would never get it back."

"We understand," said Apfel sarcastically, while von Sauerbraten shot him another look. "I'm sure you care deeply about that Israeli museum from where the pearl was stolen."

"Very true," Pancreas answered without missing a beat. The gangster sighed and leaned forward. "Two hours after I bought the pearl, my personal jeweler came by. I wanted him to design a special setting that would show off the gem in all its glory. But as I held it, it suddenly melted in my hands, causing me untold pain and some serious burns! Now I am convinced that the dealer lied to me and sold me some clever imitation."

"Can you describe this dealer in precious stones?" asked von Sauerbraten.

"Of course," said Pancreas, and gave an exact and detailed description of Big Ralph. Then he added, "Incidentally, his name is Ralph."

The two police officers could hardly contain their excitement. The junior officer stepped out of the room and returned a few minutes later with a thick photograph album.

"Please go through these photographs and point out the man who visited you," he said.

Pancreas leafed quickly through the album and without hesitation pointed to a photograph of Big Ralph.

"I don't believe it!" cried the chief. "We suspect him of being the head of a notorious gang of international criminals. The problem is that we've never been able to pin anything on him."

"What's that?" exclaimed Pancreas, pretending to be surprised. "If only I had known!" he said, striking himself on the forehead with the palm of his hand, as if annoyed at himself.

"And because you didn't call the police, we missed a chance to finally catch him in the act," chided Apfel.

"Believe me," exclaimed Pancreas, "I'm sorrier about that than you are. After all, I lost ten million dollars, and I'm the laughingstock of all my acquaintances."

There was silence in the room for a moment. Then Pancreas leaped up from his chair. "I have a way to catch that scoundrel Ralph!" he exclaimed.

"How?" asked both policemen simultaneously.

"Before I help you," said Pancreas, "I would like to know whether any help I give you will cancel out any charge you might cook up against me — concerning either what I just told you, or what I am about to tell you. I know how you boys operate. I'll be charged with withholding information, accessory to a felony, receiving stolen goods, and ten other charges when really it is I who suffered the most in this whole business."

"Who cares about that right now?" said von Sauerbraten impatiently. "Just tell us your idea about how to catch Ralph, and I'll see to it that you're not charged."

"No, no, gentlemen," exclaimed Pancreas. "It doesn't work that way. I am not satisfied with your promise. The agreement has to be written down and signed. And the agreement is that I help you find and arrest Ralph — and in return, I am not charged with anything. If asked, you will merely say that all the information I have given you was from an anonymous tip."

The chief of the Cologne police nodded to his deputy, who took out a piece of paper and wrote out an agreement. Both policemen, plus the cunning Pancreas, signed it.

"Now for pity's sake tell us how we can get him," growled von Sauerbraten.

"Okay, listen to me," said Pancreas. "Some time ago Ralph offered to sell me a painting, *Licht*, but I didn't want it."

"*Licht*?" cried the commander. "That painting was stolen from the Artothek Museum here in Cologne almost six months ago. It's considered a masterpiece of modern art."

"I know," said Pancreas, "but even if I weren't a law-abiding citizen" — another snigger from Apfel — "I wouldn't want it. In my opinion it is a doodle that any child could make. In any event, if you want to catch Ralph — may I have a pen and paper, please?" He paused and wrote a telephone number on a piece of paper, and then continued. "Just say that you are interested in *Licht*. You can say that I told you about it."

"Hmm, it's a good idea," said von Sauerbraten. "Let me think about it."

Frustrated, Pancreas pressed further. "Look, boys, if you catch Big Ralph and his gang, we will all gain. I will be doing my duty as a good German citizen, and everyone will say that it was you who managed to catch a notorious gangster and his cohorts. And who knows? Perhaps I'll get my ten million dollars back, while you'll have the arrest of the gang to your credit. It'll be great for your careers."

Von Sauerbraten looked at Apfel, and Apfel looked at von Sauerbraten. The deputy nodded slightly to his boss, who returned the gesture. "Okay," von Sauerbraten agreed. "We'll go for it."

Pancreas smiled widely. "Excellent," he said. "Gentlemen, it was a pleasure doing business with you. I wish you much luck in catching the elusive Ralph." And with that, Pancreas stood up and left.

It was quiet in the room for a few minutes. Finally, von Sauerbraten turned to his deputy. "Do you suppose we can finally borrow Bongiorno from our friends in Rome?" he asked. He was referring to Detective Captain Michelangelo Bongiorno, the Rome police department's expert on art — and one of Europe's leading tracers of stolen art, jewels, and antiques. For almost six months, the Cologne police chief had been trying to "borrow" him from the Rome police department, to help recover the stolen painting. Now with this new lead, he hoped his counterpart in Rome would finally allow Bongiorno to make a short visit to Germany.

The next morning, Detective Captain Michelangelo Bongiorno found himself on a plane to Cologne. Later that afternoon, he had a long lunch with police chief Thomas von Sauerbraten and deputy chief Konrad Apfel. By the time he was ready to walk back to his hotel, he had a piece of paper with Big Ralph's phone number in his pocket.

25

Ralph Gets Arrested

The telephone rang in Big Ralph's office. He picked it up. "Hello?"

"Hello," said the caller in Italian-accented German. "My name is Luigi Cappuccino. I'm an art and antiques dealer. I buy things in Europe for a lot of money" — Cappuccino laughed — "and sell them in America for even more. I'm looking for something in particular, and I was told you might have it."

"Talk straight. Just what is it you're after?" said Ralph.

"I have a client who wants the painting *Licht*. It doesn't matter to him how he gets it," said Cappuccino. (Of course, the caller was none other than Detective Captain Michelangelo Bongiorno, the art expert of the Rome police, and not a dealer named Cappuccino. As a matter of fact, there never was a person named Luigi Cappuccino.)

"What does that painting have to do with me? Or, rather, how did you hear about me?"

"Oh, I'm sorry. I must have made a mistake. Someone named Pancreas told me that I should talk to you about *Licht*, but it seems I got a wrong number. Please excuse me for disturbing you."

"Hold on!" cried Ralph. "You didn't make a mistake. I'm the right person for you."

"So when can I see it?" asked Bongiorno, smiling to himself.

"Saturday night, at nine o'clock, someone will meet you in front of the Kaiserhof Theater," answered Ralph. "Make sure you are wearing a yellow scarf. From the theater, you will be taken to a building in the area and shown the picture. You may examine it as carefully as you like as long as you don't harm it. If you want it, you'll pay in dollars and take it with you."

"How much?"

"Three million."

"I have to speak to my client. I'll get back to you in an hour."

As soon as he hung up, Ralph placed a call to Leopold Pancreas. Apfel had been in touch with him that morning, so Pancreas knew what to say.

"Do you know an art dealer named Cappuccino?" he asked.

Pancreas answered that he did. "He's okay," said Pancreas. "You can trust him, and you can also demand a lot of money. This client of his is loaded."

Ralph thanked Pancreas and told him he would be happy return the favor whenever Pancreas asked. "I'll be seeing you," said the former fake priest to Ralph — but to himself he laughed, thinking that his favor was going to cost Ralph a lot more than he thought.

Within half an hour, Bongiorno was on the line again. "Hello. I spoke to my client, and he is willing to pay two-and-a-half million."

"No way," said Ralph. "I've decided not to sell for less than five million."

"I don't understand. Half an hour ago, you asked for only three million."

"Yes, but the price just went up in the last half hour. I have other clients, too. I'm certainly not desperate."

"Lower the price or the deal is off," said Bongiorno. (Of course, he was planning to arrest Ralph, not pay him, but he had to bargain so he would sound like a real buyer.)

"Okay. I'll come down to four," said Ralph.

"Three."

"Four, and not a cent less."

"Three-and-a-half," pressed Bongiorno.

"Good-bye," said Ralph. "I'm not a fishmonger. I won't be nickled-and-dimed by you."

Bongiorno gave in. "Okay, okay, four million. I'll be at the theater on Saturday night."

Twenty minutes later, Bongiorno was in von Sauerbraten's office. He repeated his conversation with Ralph to the police chief. Von Sauerbraten called Apfel to come in, and the three of them started planning the operation.

*   *   *

Michelangelo Bongiorno arrived at the Kaiserhof Theater at exactly nine o'clock Saturday night. Attached to his yellow scarf was a tiny tracking device so the police could follow his movements. In the street near the theater were five plain-clothes policemen waiting for the word from Bongiorno. An unmarked squad car was parked a few blocks away.

A tall, thin man came up to Bongiorno. "Mr. Cappuccino?" he asked. Bongiorno nodded. "I am Carlo. I work for Ralph. Come with me, please. I will take you to see the painting."

Bongiorno followed the man to a nondescript-looking building around the corner. They ascended two flights of stairs. The man opened the door to one of the apartments, and the two men entered. Unbeknownst to Carlo, the plain-clothesmen had followed them and were taking their places near the building.

Once inside, Bongiorno was led into a room with a locked steel door, and the door was then locked from the in-side. On the wall hung a framed picture — a rather mediocre Paris street scene. Bongiorno looked puzzled. Carlo laughed. He turned the picture to the wall and carefully peeled off the brown paper that covered the back of the picture. The glorious colors of *Licht* were suddenly revealed. Bongiorno inhaled sharply. He examined the picture carefully for a long time. Finally he nodded and said, "Yes, it's authentic."

"What about the money?" asked Carlo.

"My assistant has it. He's back at the theater. I'll call him and tell him to meet me at the corner." Bongiorno whipped out a cell phone.

Carlo said, "You won't get any reception in here. I'll take you to the entrance hall."

Bongiorno examined the picture carefully for a long time.

The two men went back to the apartment's entrance. Bongiorno punched in some numbers on his cell phone and when the other party answered, said, "Okay. Get the money ready and meet me at the north end of the street, on the first corner."

This was the call the plainclothesmen were waiting for. They burst into the apartment and arrested Carlo.

*   *   *

When questioned by the police, Carlo revealed enough about Ralph's present whereabouts for von Sauerbraten and Apfel to get on his trail. By three o'clock in the morning, he was arrested. He was so surprised that for five minutes he could only stammer and sputter. The next day, Ralph, his lawyer, and two detectives were sitting in a small office. Ralph was anxious to enter into a plea-bargaining agreement. Therefore, within a few hours, the detectives knew all about Dr. Bloch's kidnapping and Sigmund Kranker's part in the theft of the Red Pearl.

"Where is the real Red Pearl now?" asked one of the detectives.

"What do you mean, the real Red Pearl? Haven't you been listening? Kranker stole it from the museum, and I stole it from Bloch's brother because that idiot Hochstadt gave it to him thinking he was Kranker. Then I sold it. That's the only Red Pearl there ever was."

"That's a lie." The detective turned to his colleague. "Let Pancreas in," he said. The door was opened and Leopold Pancreas entered. "What do you say?" asked the detective.

"You sold me a red pearl, true enough," said Pancreas to Ralph, "but not the real one. You sold me some kind of a fake — it melted in my hands two hours after I bought it!"

"Ahh!" cried Ralph in rage. "Now I know where the real pearl is. That must be it."

"What must be it, and where's the pearl?" asked the detective impatiently.

"Obviously, Sigmund Kranker has it. He betrayed me! The pearl he stole he kept for himself, and gave me a fake instead. You know he's a famous magician. He knows a million tricks."

After some telephoning here and there, the Cologne police found out where Sigmund Kranker's circus was camped. The next evening, they were on their way to arrest him.

26

Gazlano Goes to Jail

The audience cheered and applauded as Gazlano the Great finished his performance, bowed graciously, and then stepped out of the circus tent. He could hear the applause fading away as he walked toward his trailer.

As he was putting his key into the lock a voice said from behind him, "Good evening, Dr. Bloch."

Sigmund turned around and saw two policemen.

"Ha!" said one of the policemen. "What do you say, Mr. Kranker — or should I say Gazlano? You have a very convenient way of changing names."

Sigmund felt the way he had when the man in the museum was pointing the gun at him.

"May I ask what you want?" he said in a shaking voice.

"You are under arrest!" said the other policeman.

"For what?" asked Sigmund, feeling his voice betray him.

"You are wanted by the Israeli police for questioning regarding both the kidnapping of Dr. Raphael Bloch of Haifa, Israel, and the theft of a red pearl from the museum of which

Dr. Bloch is the director. You are being arrested at their request, but we have arranged to question you — and, if need
be, prosecute you — here in Germany."

"What in the world are you talking about?" cried Sigmund angrily. "Search anywhere you want. I don't have any
pearl."

"We didn't come to argue with you. Here is the arrest
warrant. Pack your personal belongings and come with us."

Sigmund went into his trailer. He put what he would
need in a small suitcase. He hesitated for a moment, and
then opened a drawer and took out the photograph of the
triplets and put that in, too. Then he told the police that he
was ready to go.

"We have a warrant to search your trailer," said one of the
policemen. "Two of our colleagues are on the way here. But
you'll make it easier on all of us if you bring the pearl with
you now."

Sigmund didn't answer. He asked permission to say good-
bye to the director of the circus, and the police accompanied
him to the director's office. Then Sigmund followed them to
their car.

$*$ $*$ $*$

On the way to the Cologne police station, Sigmund remembered the letter that the Bloch brothers sent him. They
had written, "… you don't have to go into hiding or be afraid
of the police. We have no intention of reporting you, even
though if we did we might get the pearl back. You are dearer
to us than all the pearls in the world."

Sigmund sighed and thought, "Brothers or doubles; either way — liars! They did inform on me. How else could the police know about my part in the affair of the pearl?" It didn't occur to Sigmund that Ralph had been caught and that it was he who had informed on him.

When Sigmund arrived at the police station, he was taken to an office where a policeman asked him questions and filled out forms. Another policeman then took his fingerprints. One at a time, his fingers were pressed first on a pad with black ink and then on one of the forms the policeman had filled out. Sigmund vaguely remembered that he had done that once before, But when… and why?

After being fingerprinted and told to call a lawyer, he was taken to a room for questioning. Fifteen minutes later, a detective entered holding a manilla envelope. The detective had decided to speak candidly with him. "Good evening, Mr. Kranker," he said. "I thought we'd have a little chat before you meet with your lawyer. It might help you understand what's going on.

"First of all, I'll tell you how we got on your trail — perhaps that will make you want to cooperate with us. Cooperation will mean a lighter sentence, although I imagine that you won't get less than five years in prison. On the other hand, if you don't cooperate, you might get twice as much."

Sigmund bit his lip, and the detective began to tell him the whole story of the theft of the Red Pearl in Israel. "…And so, you turned the pearl over to the person you know as Ralph, or Big Ralph. He sold it to a resident of Cologne. A few hours later, the stone melted, giving the buyer serious burns. That person called us, and with his help we managed to nab Ralph. He told us how you took Dr. Bloch's place. But you were even more clever than Ralph! You gave him a fake pearl and kept the real one for yourself. So, my first question is, Where is the real Red Pearl?"

Sigmund realized that in fact Dr. Bloch had kept his promise; he had not made a complaint to the police about him — and, it seemed, would not. It looked as if the police were relying entirely on what Ralph said.

He looked straight at the detective and exploded, "That is the most ridiculous thing I ever heard! Do you mean to tell me that you are relying on what the boss of a criminal gang told you? The whole thing is lies from beginning to end. I never pretended to be Dr. Bloch. Did he tell the police that he had been kidnapped? Call him and ask him — that is, if he really exists — and you will see that the whole thing is completely and utterly false."

"In other words," said the detective, "you completely deny the story?"

"It's all a lie!" yelled Sigmund, feeling that he had outsmarted his interrogator.

The detective reached into the manilla envelope and took out Sigmund's passport. He thumbed through it and then held it up so Sigmund could see it, pointing to the dates that had been stamped in it at the airport when Sigmund had entered and left Israel. "This was found when we searched your trailer. Please be kind enough to explain to me what you were doing in Israel at the time the pearl was stolen," he said.

"I was there as a tourist."

"And how do you explain a million-dollar transfer from a Swiss bank to your account here in Cologne — the day after you returned to Germany?"

"I don't have to explain anything without my lawyer," said Sigmund.

"You're a tough nut to crack," said the detective angrily. "Where did you hide the Red Pearl?"

"I didn't steal it, and so it isn't in my possession," said Sigmund with confidence.

"Fine. We'll wait for your lawyer to show up. But allow me to read you a statement by a trustworthy and reliable person who accuses you of helping kidnap Dr. Bloch and steal the Red Pearl."

"Who is this person?" asked Sigmund.

"You yourself," said the detective solemnly, and took a handwritten letter out of the envelope.

When he saw the letter, Sigmund's face turned white and his knees shook.

Of course, this was the letter that Sigmund had put in his safe deposit box before he left for Israel — with instructions to the manager of the bank to open the box if he wasn't back within four months. Sigmund had even told Ralph about the letter, so that Ralph wouldn't be tempted to harm him. Ralph remembered this very well. In his desire to take revenge on Sigmund, Ralph told the police about the letter. After all, Ralph thought, Sigmund had cheated him by giving him a fake pearl.

To Sigmund's great sorrow, the letter was still in the safe deposit box when the police went to the bank. Sigmund had intended to take the letter back as soon as possible, but he hadn't done it yet. The police must have gotten a court order to open the box. It was this letter that the detective proceeded to read aloud.

This is what it said:

To the police: For your information, I, Sigmund Kranker, and the gang led by a man known as Big Ralph, will be leaving soon for Israel. The gang intends to kidnap a Dr. Raphael Bloch, director of the Haifa Maritime Museum. I will then impersonate Dr. Bloch and steal the Red Pearl from the museum. Then I will deliver it to Ralph.

Because I am afraid that Ralph will want to harm me, I am leaving this letter in my safe deposit box. If this letter reaches you, please be advised that Ralph has the Red Pearl.

Sigmund Kranker

"What do you say about such trustworthy evidence?" asked the detective stonily.

Sigmund didn't answer.

"You were suspicious of Ralph, but it turns out that you cheated him. You gave him a fake stone that dissolved, whereas the real pearl you kept." The detective changed his tone and spoke softly, "I am appealing to you: For your own sake, tell me where the pearl is."

"Sir," said Sigmund to the policeman, "it's true that I lied to you. I was in Israel to impersonate the head of the Haifa Maritime Museum, and I stole the Red Pearl. But I turned it over to Ralph. It may be that we didn't steal the real Red Pearl at all. I don't have another pearl, and I can't confess to something I didn't do."

"I am asking you for the last time," said the detective angrily. "*Where is the real Red Pearl?*"

"Believe me, I don't have it," insisted Sigmund.

"You really are stubborn!" cried the detective. He picked up the phone and punched in a few numbers. "Get in here and take Mr. Kranker to his cell."

Sigmund was taken to a cell. As he passed the room where his fingerprints had been taken, the question once again troubled him: "Where did I have my fingerprints taken, and by whom?"

Sigmund suddenly remembered the package he had received from the Bloch brothers. Enclosed had been a photocopy of Raphael Bloch's fingerprint notebook. The brothers had claimed that it contained Sigmund's fingerprints.

A memory illuminated Sigmund's brain for an instant: He was dipping his fingers in black ink and pressing them onto a piece of paper. Where, oh where, was that memory from?

The memory faded as quickly as it had come. Sigmund sat on the bed in his cell, ate the meager supper that the jailer brought him, and fell asleep, tired and drained.

27

Afikomen Presents

Thirty-four years earlier, Pesach Sheini 5719.

"Oh! Thank you, Abba!" cried Rafi as he opened his *afikomen* present. It was the Blochs' custom to give the *afikomen* presents on Pesach Sheini. "Aharon! Moishy! Look — Abba got me the fingerprint ink I asked for! Tomorrow I'll buy a notebook and take everybody's fingerprints. What did you get, Aharon?"

"A *Kitzur Shulchan Aruch*, just what I asked for," answered Aharon. "Thank you, Imma and Abba."

The boy's father smiled with satisfaction. He was very happy that his nine-year-old son wanted *sifrei kodesh*.

"And Moishy," asked Rafi, "did you get the bowling game you wanted?"

"No," answered Moishy, and looked at his father with a half-smile.

His father smiled, too, and stroked Moishy's cheek. Two days before, the boys' rebbe had told them about missionaries and about Yad l'Achim, an organization that fights missionary activity in Eretz Yisrael. What the teacher said had made a strong impression on Moishy, and after school he told his father that he wanted to give the money for his *afikomen* present to Yad l'Achim.

"You are a real *tzaddik*," his father had said, and Moishy felt his heart fill with happiness.

*   *   *

The year 5753, at night in a cell in a Cologne jail.

The smile on the face of the sleeping Sigmund was completely out of place, considering his sad circumstances. A person who saw him would probably think that he was having a happy dream. And he was.

In the dream, a Jewish boy showed him a black bottle and said happily, "Look, Moishy! See what I got for the *afikomen*? Fingerprint ink! Let me take your fingerprints for my notebook."

In his dream, Sigmund chuckled and said to the Jewish boy, "You're mistaken, Raphael. I'm not Moishy. It's very nice that you got a fingerprint kit for the *auch gekommen*, but I don't want to get my fingers dirty."

Suddenly the Jewish boy was dressed as a policeman and said in a harsh voice, "Stop being stubborn! Put your fingers on the ink pad."

In the dream a child's voice was heard, saying, "But Rafi, why did you say black ink? Uncle Moishy's hands are in the white plaster mixture. He helped me stick the tile back on the kitchen baseboard."

Sigmund dreamed that he then looked at his hands, and it was true — his fingers were not black, but white. "What happened, Rafi?" he asked. "How did the black on my fingers turn white?"

Suddenly Rafi disappeared, and a man appeared, smiling happily. "Don't you understand, my Moishy? The black turned to white. Don't you remember that you gave the money for your *afikomen* present to Yad l'Achim? They save people from the missionaries, so they won't have black *neshamos*. They will remain Jews with white *neshamos*. You are a *tzaddik*, Moishy!"

"Are you my father?" asked Sigmund.

"Of course I'm your father," answered the man.

"Then, father, maybe you can explain why there are pearls that melt?"

"That's the way things are in this world," said the man — but suddenly, he had the voice of Rabbi Aharon Bloch. "Everyone chases after things that dissolve, or that become disgusting, like an egg in coffee. The Torah and the *mitzvos* are the only pearls that never disintegrate."

Sigmund held out his hand to the man and said, "Come again to visit. And please don't tell anyone about the donation."

To his surprise, Sigmund woke up in the morning with a pleasant feeling. At the same time, he was puzzled by the dream. He was surprised to have remembered that in fact he had once left his fingerprints in a Jewish boy's notebook.

*   *   *

Throughout his repeated interrogations by the police — this time in the presence of his lawyer — Sigmund stubbornly maintained that he had no pearl. Finally, the case was turned over to the public prosecutor.

Meanwhile, all that remained of Pancreas's unpleasant incident with Big Ralph were two small burn marks on his cheeks.

Three days after Sigmund's arrest, an interesting news item was reported in the *Kölnische Rundschau*, one of Cologne's largest newspapers. It said that the trial of the famous Gazlano the Great — also known as Sigmund Kranker — was scheduled to start in three weeks.

Rumor had it that if Kranker hadn't been so stubborn, and had revealed where the real Red Pearl was, he would have made things much easier for himself. But he kept on insisting that he didn't have the real pearl.

Sigmund's lawyer began to build the defense.

28

The Brothers' Efforts

The telephone rang and Dr. Ph. Litmus picked it up. "Hello?" he said.

"Hello, Dr. Litmus. This is Raphael Bloch speaking."

"Yes, Dr. Bloch. What can I do for you?"

"I need your help, Dr. Litmus, and I have to ask you, even though it will involve something that may be unpleasant. I'm sorry to say that the man who stole the pearl you cooked up has been caught."

"You're sorry?" asked Litmus in surprise.

"I am indeed," answered Raphael Bloch. "The unfortunate thief is none other than my brother, Sigmund Kranker — or Gazlano the Great, as he is called."

Litmus was amazed. "The famous magician Gazlano the Great is your brother?"

"He is, and when I have a chance I'll tell you all about it. Right now, however, I want to get back to the matter in which I need your help."

"I'm all ears," said Litmus.

"Well, my brother Gazlano — Sigmund — impersonated me at the museum, and because we look so much alike, everyone thought that he was I. That's how my poor brother managed to steal the pearl. After he took it, he delivered it to the gang of crooks who hired him. They sold the pearl, but then it melted — as you knew it would — and the buyer called the police. To make a long story short, my brother was arrested at the same time as some of the gang members."

"I'm very upset to hear that," said Litmus, "but what is it that I can do to help you?"

"It's really very simple," answered Dr. Bloch. "The police believe that my brother turned a fake pearl over to the gang, and that he has the real one hidden somewhere. What really makes them angry is that my brother is unwilling to tell them where the real Red Pearl is. Neither the police nor my brother even imagine that there never really was a Red Pearl."

"Just a minute," interrupted Litmus, "why are the police accusing your brother of having turned over a fake pearl to the crooks? Why don't they suspect the head of the gang? Why don't they think that he got the real pearl from your brother, but sold his customer a fake?"

"I looked into that," answered Bloch. "The police think my brother could make an imitation pearl because he is well-known for his tricks. They don't give the gang credit for that much intelligence."

"So what would you like me to do?" asked Litmus.

Bloch sighed. "I don't see any other way, Dr. Litmus. We need you to be a witness for the defense in my brother's trial. You'll have to testify that you cooked up the pearl yourself, making it so it would decompose in three months' time, and then sent it to me. That may be enough to acquit my brother. At least it should get him a lighter sentence. The court can't punish him for stealing and keeping a stolen jewel if what he stole wasn't really a jewel and doesn't exist anymore."

The telephone was silent for a long time. Finally Litmus said, "I will testify. It will be all right."

"I am very, very grateful to you, Dr. Litmus," said Bloch. "Your testimony should be enough to have the charge of theft dismissed. However, we will also need you to cook up a fake pearl on the witness stand, which will disintegrate after a certain period of time. This means, of course, that you will have to reveal your method and ingredients."

"I understand and I am willing," said Litmus.

"Wonderful." Bloch sighed. "That would leave only the charge of being an accessory to kidnapping."

"Kidnapping?" said Litmus in surprise.

"Yes. I was kidnapped by the gang and my brother took my place. But I hope to be allowed to testify, and I will say that I completely forgive my brother and didn't complain to the police. I hope and pray that things will be all right."

"When and where is the trial?"

"In about three weeks, in Cologne, Germany."

"Fine. I'll come to Cologne in two-and-a-half weeks. I'll let you know where I'll be staying, and we'll be in touch then."

"Thank you, Dr. Litmus. I am very grateful to you," said Dr. Bloch, and hung up the phone.

*   *   *

Sigmund was afraid. The window in his cell didn't close properly, and from time to time a bee flew in. He shivered in fear. Finally he couldn't stand it anymore. He banged as hard as he could on the door of his cell until he heard footsteps approaching.

The pass-through window in the door of the cell was opened and the guard's face appeared. "What do you want?" he asked in a bored voice.

"I can't take this! Bees are flying in and out of the window all the time," cried Sigmund in anger and fear. "Put me in a cell that has a window I can close," he pleaded.

"Bees?" said the guard. "You'll have to get used to it. There's a beehive not far away. As for the window, the prisoner who was in here before you jammed it and we haven't had time to fix it."

"I demand to be moved to another cell!" cried Sigmund. "I can't stand it here with the bees."

"You're a funny one, you and your bees."

"Please! Pass on to the officer in charge my request to be moved."

"We don't move people because of bees."

Sigmund started to say something about moving because of a broken window, but the pass-through was slammed shut and Sigmund heard the jailer's footsteps receding down the corridor.

"God in Heaven!" whispered Sigmund, and tears rolled down his cheeks. "God in Heaven, have pity on me! I don't know who I am or why a tiny bee fills me with such terror. I feel like a little boy who is going to prison because of some

"I can't take this! Bees are flying in and out of the window all the time."

mischief he did. Dear God in Heaven…" Sigmund lay sobbing on the bed for a long time.

The day was like one long nightmare. Sigmund held his towel all the time, and whenever a bee flew into his cell he stood tensely, gripping his towel, ready to ward off the bee if it came close.

In the afternoon, four bees flew in the window one after another and buzzed lazily around the cell. They probably would have left just as they came if Sigmund hadn't started swatting with his towel in every direction like a man gone mad.

The bees were alarmed and circled around Sigmund. Sigmund whirled his towel. Whack! Two bees fell to the floor dead. Whack! Whack! Another bee flew out the window, but the fourth landed on Sigmund's neck and stung him.

"Nooooo!" A terrified shriek burst from Sigmund. He closed his eyes, staggered a few steps, fainted, and fell to the floor. As he lost consciousness, he felt as if he were falling and falling and falling and falling… Strange sights passed before his eyes, sights that carried him back thirty-three years, to the day when he tumbled down the slippery hillside and fell into the river.

*   *   *

Everyone in police headquarters heard Sigmund's blood-curdling scream. The guard who had earlier slammed the pass-through window in Sigmund's face came pounding down the corridor to his cell. He opened the door and saw Sigmund lying on the floor unconscious. He ran to his telephone. A few minutes later, two paramedics came dashing down the hall with a stretcher and carried Sigmund to the prison infirmary.

The doctor who examined him could find no sign of anything that could explain what happened. "Leave him to awaken by himself," he told the paramedics. "If he gets worse or if he doesn't wake up within an hour, he'll need to be taken to the hospital."

In the meantime, the unconscious Sigmund continued to fall…

"When will the end of this fall come?" he thought in his dream. He heard Aharon and Raphael calling him and saw them standing high on the hill. Then he looked down…

His father and mother were waiting for him, holding a thick mattress piled high with cotton, to break his fall.

Suddenly he saw himself lying in bed, with his father and mother standing at the bedside.

"Abba, Imma, I promise you I'll become a good boy, like Aharon," he said in his dream.

"Nu," said his father, "every mitzvah brings another. First *tzedakah*, and then Torah."

Suddenly he heard Raphael and Aharon asking if he was all right.

His father answered them: "He's perfectly all right, and with Hashem's help he'll be even better."

Sigmund wanted to open his eyes, but he heard another voice, this one hoarse and rough, saying, "He's waking up. He's okay."

"Very good," said another voice, and Sigmund didn't want to open his eyes anymore, because he recognized that voice:

It was the detective who had interrogated him endlessly.

Finally he opened his eyes and looked around in puzzlement. Then he sighed: he understood that his conversation with his family had been only a dream.

"Are you okay?" asked the detective.

"Perfectly okay," answered Sigmund.

"So what happened that made you suddenly scream and faint?"

"Sometimes things just happen suddenly," answered Sigmund calmly.

"I understand that you wanted to be moved to another cell."

"I did, but not anymore." Sigmund himself was surprised by these words, but felt that now he could even hold a bee in his hand without fear.

"Hmm. Okay, if you have any other requests, ask the guard to call me."

"I do have one request. Can you tell me my name?"

The detective looked at Sigmund in astonishment and finally said, "Your name is Sigmund Kranker."

"Are you sure of that? Please, check my papers again. It seems to me that my name may be Moshe Sigmund."

The detective looked at Sigmund worriedly and gave orders to have him moved to a better cell.

During the time that remained until his trial, foggy memories of Sigmund's childhood came back to him. But one thing he couldn't fathom: Could it be possible that Peter and Irena had kidnapped him? And yet, how could he even think such a thing?

29
Sigmund's Trial

The courtroom was packed and buzzing. The fame of the acclaimed magician Gazlano the Great had attracted a large audience to his trial.

Among the witnesses for the prosecution were Leopold Pancreas, the detective who had interrogated Sigmund, two members of Big Ralph's gang, and the aged Dr. Gustav von Holzwald (who had been chairman of the archaeological congress at which the Red Pearl had been revealed to the world). The prosecuting attorney was none other than Mr. Ernst Kutschma, a well-known public prosecutor.

The defense witnesses included the director of the Baldini Circus, Dr. Raphael Bloch (who surprised everyone by appearing for the defense rather than the prosecution), the messenger who delivered the fake pearl to Dr. Bloch in Haifa, the world-famous chemist Dr. Ph. Litmus (whose reason for appearing no one knew), and an expert on gems. Rumor had it that there might be another couple of witnesses for the defense as well.

The murmur of the crowd ended as the judge came in and took his place.

The judge put on a grave expression, faced Sigmund, and asked, "Are you Sigmund Kranker?"

"I am the person called by that name," answered Sigmund.

The judge rolled his eyes. "Sigmund Kranker," the judge continued, "you are accused of theft, concealing stolen property, and being an accessory to kidnapping. Do you understand the charges against you?"

"Yes I do, your honor."

"How do you plead?"

"I plead guilty to being an accessory to the kidnapping of Dr. Bloch, in that I impersonated him while he was being held by Big Ralph's gang. I plead guilty to the theft of the Red Pearl. I plead not guilty to the charge of concealing stolen property. I deny that I kept the pearl and passed on an imitation to the gang. What I stole, I delivered to the gang, and there is no Red Pearl in my possession."

The judge nodded to the prosecutor, who rose to make his opening speech.

"Your honor," he said, "approximately two months ago an agreement was reached between the accused, Sigmund Kranker, and Ralph Ripoff, also known as Big Ralph. Big Ralph, by the way, was recently unmasked as the head of an international gang of criminals. Anyway, the accused agreed to steal the famous Red Pearl from the Maritime Museum in Haifa, Israel, by impersonating the director of the museum, Dr. Raphael Bloch — and to turn the pearl over to Ripoff. In return, Ripoff would give the accused a large sum of money.

"It is true that the accused — who bears a remarkable resemblance to Dr. Bloch — was not directly involved in the kidnapping. He merely impersonated Dr. Bloch, who was held captive by the criminals. But if the accused had not impersonated Dr. Bloch, the police would have been called in immediately after he had been missing from the museum for a day. Therefore the accused, by impersonating Dr. Bloch, prevented the discovery of the kidnapping, and he should be treated as severely as if he were one of the kidnappers.

"There is no need for us to prove that the accused stole the Red Pearl since he admitted doing it. However, when he was first questioned by the police, the accused denied any connection with the kidnapping and robbery. He admitted his part in the affair only after he was shown proof of his complicity in the form of a letter found in his safe deposit box in the Kölnische Shimmelbank." The prosecutor handed the letter to the judge.

The judge studied the letter and motioned for the prosecutor to continue. "Now I will turn to the third charge against Kranker. We maintain that the accused still has the stolen pearl. Therefore, he shows that not only does he not repent at all for what he did, but actually continues his act of theft. We maintain that the accused delivered a false pearl to Ralph Ripoff and his gang, while keeping the real one for himself. Regarding that, we will hear the testimony of Mr. Leopold Pancreas."

It was then the defense attorney's turn to speak. He kept his remarks brief, emphasizing that Sigmund Kranker had never been in trouble with the law before. He made mention of the infamous gang leader Big Ralph and his upcoming trial for theft and kidnapping. And he wondered out loud whether Ralph himself couldn't have switched the real Red Pearl for a fake one, and passed it on to Pancreas.

Soon enough it was time for the prosecution to call its first witness. Mr. Leopold Pancreas got up and walked to the witness stand.

As soon as Pancreas began to speak, Sigmund frowned. His voice and appearance reminded him of something from his past. Sigmund tried to remember, but he couldn't.

The same frown appeared on the faces of both Dr. Raphael Bloch and his brother Rabbi Aharon Bloch, who were sitting among the spectators. They both knew that they had seen that face before, and tried in vain to remember where and when. The name Pancreas also reminded them of something from their childhood. Both of them knew it had to do with the town in the Catskills where the Bloch family had spent their summer vacations.

"About a month ago," said Pancreas with some hesitation, "a man came to my house and offered to sell me a red pearl for a very large sum of money. Needless to say, I immediately suspected that the man was trying to sell me the pearl that had been stolen not long before, but he convinced me that it was a different one. He made a good impression on me, and I told myself that there must be many red pearls in the world.

"To make a long story short, I thought the stone really was a genuine red pearl, so I paid what the anonymous seller asked. But two hours later the pearl melted in my hand. I contacted the police and gave an exact description of the man who had sold me the pearl. With my description, the police succeeded in catching him and others in his gang, who had stolen the pearl from the museum in Israel. When questioned, they said that the person who had given them the pearl was none other than the famous magician Gazlano the Great — or Sigmund Kranker. And now we know that he betrayed them and gave them a false pearl, and kept the real one for himself."

"Objection, your honor!" cried Sigmund's lawyer. "The witness's last statement is pure hearsay and I request that it be stricken from the record."

"Objection sustained," said the judge. "Mr. Kutschma," he said, turning to the prosecuting attorney, "do you have any actual proof that the accused kept the real pearl for himself and turned over an imitation to the gang? Isn't it possible that he gave the gang the real pearl, and they swindled Mr. Pancreas by selling him a fake? Maybe the real pearl is still in their possession."

"Your honor," answered the prosecutor, "an ordinary person would not be able to make an imitation pearl that was indistinguishable from the real thing and that would suddenly melt and evaporate. But Sigmund Kranker is a world-famous conjurer, with an enormous repertoire of tricks. In fact, at one of his performances I saw with my own eyes how he made a small ball vanish into thin air while he was holding it up for the audience to see. Therefore, the chances are that he is the one who has the pearl."

The judge interrupted the prosecutor. "Must I point out," he said a little sharply, "that what the court wants is proof, not probability? You have given us no clear proof that the accused turned over a fake pearl to the gang. Do you have more witnesses?" he asked.

The prosecutor said he did, and called the detective of the Cologne police who had interrogated Sigmund. He droned on for twenty minutes. Then the two members of Big Ralph's gang took the stand one after the other. They had been promised immunity from prosecution if they testified against both Sigmund and Ralph, and they were anxious to do their civic duty.

Finally, the prosecuting attorney called the last witness for the prosecution, Dr. Gustav von Holzwald. The aged scientist shuffled to the witness stand, but when he reached it he burst into an impassioned speech even before the prosecutor could ask his first question. "I demand that the accused be given the maximum sentence!" he exclaimed. "I demand that he be forced to reveal where he has hidden the real Red Pearl. Your honor, this was not an ordinary robbery. Kranker didn't steal just a pearl. He stole invaluable scientific evidence! He committed a crime against the whole world! I am astonished that Dr. Bloch is among the witnesses for the defense. I cannot understand how a scientist can defend such a crime against science..."

The judge had been trying to interrupt von Holzwald, and finally succeeded. "Dr. von Holzwald," he said, "as a witness, you are supposed to answer questions, not make speeches. I presume the prosecuting attorney will ask you what is the scientific importance of the Red Pearl, and then you can tell us briefly. But…"

Dr. von Holzwald's whole body had begun to tremble. His doctor, who had accompanied him to the trial, hurried to the bench and asked the judge to excuse the old man from testifying. "Your honor, in my opinion Dr. von Holzwald's testifying will actually endanger his life," he explained. The judge nodded in agreement — to the chagrin of the prosecutor — and the doctor took von Holzwald's elbow and guided him back to his seat.

Kutschma informed the judge that he had no more witnesses, and asked him to find Kranker guilty of all charges and give him a heavy sentence.

*   *   *

Now it was time for the defense to plead their case. Sigmund's attorney, whose name was Stan von Himmel, stood up to call his witnesses. First came the director of the circus, who gave heartwarming testimony as to the integrity and good character of the accused. Then came Dr. Bloch. He explained in a frightening combination of Yiddish and German how the pearl came into his possession and where it was placed in the museum. After him, the messenger who delivered the pearl to Dr. Bloch testified that he received the pearl from the famous chemist, Dr. Ph. Litmus, in Belgium and delivered it to Dr. Bloch in Haifa. A murmur went through the courtroom.

Von Himmel then addressed the court. "Your honor," he began, "I wish to refute the ridiculous charge that the

Red Pearl is still in the possession of my client, Sigmund Kranker. The pearl that Kranker took from the museum he gave to the criminals. To prove this, we will now call Dr. Ph. Litmus."

Dr. Litmus was somewhat agitated as he stood up and took his place in the witness stand. The defense attorney motioned for him to speak. "Gentlemen," he said in fluent but French-accented German, "I must ask your pardon, and" — here he looked at the aged archaeologist — "yours in particular, Dr. von Holzwald." He took a deep breath and continued. "I do not know whether somewhere in the depths of the sea there is a red pearl, or whether there never was such a thing. The experts have argued about this question and thrashed it out endlessly."

Dr. von Holzwald jumped to his feet and burst out, "What are you talking about? What was it that Dr. Bloch showed us at the Geneva congress, if not a red pearl? What was stolen from the museum — what is this trial all about — if not the Red Pearl?"

The judge told von Holzwald to sit down, and warned him sternly, "With all due respect, Dr. von Holzwald, if there is another outburst like that from you, I will have to order you removed from the courtroom."

Before continuing, Litmus turned to the judge and said in a low voice, "What I am about to say will undoubtedly make him very angry. Perhaps for his own sake he should go out. At least, his doctor should monitor him very carefully."

The judge repeated to von Holzwald what Litmus had said. "I'm not leaving!" von Holzwald growled.

"But no outbursts!" cautioned the judge, and then told Litmus to continue.

Litmus cleared his throat and said, "So, as I said, time will tell whether the Red Pearl is a dream or reality, but one thing is clear: the pearl that Dr. Bloch had, the one he showed at the Geneva congress, is no pearl at all, but an outright fake, made by a very simple process out of materials every chemist is familiar with."

"How dare you!" bellowed von Holzwald, brushing off his doctor's hand and leaping to his feet. But Litmus ignored him. "Moreover," he continued, "the person who made this fake — a forgery so good that it fooled the entire scientific community — this deceiving forger, I tell you, is none other than I myself. This will be proven in a moment. But first, I have something interesting to show the court." Litmus reached into his jacket pocket and took out a small red sphere. Holding it up so that everyone in the room could see, he said, "Here is a pearl that is identical to the one that was entrusted to Dr. Bloch." He reached into his pocket again and took out another red pearl, and another, and another... As the astounded crowd watched, Litmus lined up ten red pearls on the table.

"These will last a few weeks," he said, "and then they will melt, as did the other pearl. For it was I who sent the pearl anonymously to Dr. Bloch." Litmus stood up and prepared to leave the witness stand.

"Litmus, you counterfeiter! You crook! You misled the whole scientific world!" screamed von Holzwald in rage.

At this point, the judge finally lost his patience. "Dr. von

Holzwald, I must ask you to leave immediately. You have disrupted this trial too many times."

As a livid von Holzwald was helped to his feet by his doctor, Litmus stood up. He looked von Holzwald straight in the eye.

"Professor von Holzwald," said Litmus calmly. "I was involved in an interesting investigation. I asked myself: "Is every conclusion drawn by the scientific world absolutely true? Or perhaps scientists — whom you regard so highly — can also make mistakes. Perhaps they can draw incorrect conclusions — even when they solemnly declare that something is a fact beyond question.

"For this interesting research," continued Litmus, "I made the Red Pearl, and the experiment succeeded beyond my wildest expectations. Why? Because from now on, every statement that scientists make will be seen by the public as only a hypothesis — and not as something 100 percent true and unquestionable! Was I not right, then, to perform this experiment?"

Litmus looked straight at von Holzwald, but the latter made no reply. His face was white, and his whole body shook with rage. His doctor hurried him out of the courtroom. "The pearl that Dr. Bloch had," resumed Litmus, "was prepared from ordinary chemicals of no particular value, and nothing else. And to prove this, I will prepare a red pearl while you watch. I will use my exact recipe, except I will add an accelerating ingredient so that the pearl will be ready in only a few minutes and will last only about two minutes before melting. I would like Dr. Bloch to examine it before it melts and

"I will prepare a red pearl while you watch. It will last only about two minutes before melting."

confirm that it is just like the pearl he had. I also understand that an expert on gems will examine the pearl as well."

The room was quiet, and every eye was on Litmus. He opened a briefcase and took out a large test tube, some tongs, and a number of small bottles. Meanwhile a court clerk brought a table to the witness stand along with an electric hot plate and a pot. These he placed on the table.

The chemist emptied the bottles into the test tube, then boiled the test tube for a few minutes in the pot. After this he added a few drops from another bottle until the mixture became dark red. He then added some powder to the mixture. At this point he looked up and said, "The powder is an accelerator. As you can see, I use no special equipment except for the test tube, and tongs to handle it with when it gets hot. Moreover, the materials I use can be found in almost any laboratory. Now…" He took a small brown envelope out of the briefcase, tore open the corner, and shook some powder from the envelope into the test tube. He swirled the test tube and said, "The longer one waits now, the larger the pearl will become. But I don't want to keep everyone waiting, so — first we get rid of what we don't want, then…"

Litmus poured a clear liquid into the pot. The courtroom was so still that one could have heard a pin drop. He tipped the test tube… and a small red pearl fell into his palm. He picked it up and gave it to the judge. "Here's your Red Pearl!" he declared.

The spectators, who until then had been sitting in absolute silence, burst into wild applause. The defense attorney took the pearl from the judge and said, "We must hurry and examine this fake pearl before it dissolves. Dr. Bloch, please come down here and tell us if this is like the pearl you had."

Bloch examined the pearl carefully with a strong magnifying glass before answering, "Yes, as far as I can tell without laboratory tests, this object is identical to the one the messenger brought me — only smaller," he said.

Von Himmel then called the expert on gems to come to the witness stand and examine the pearl as well. A short, fat man hurriedly got up and made his way down the aisle.

Bloch handed him the pearl, and the expert took out a jeweler's monocle. He, too, scrutinized it carefully and then said, "Yes, if I didn't know better, I would say that this is a 100 percent, genuine pearl."

The chemist carefully took the fake pearl, put it on a saucer, and said, "Not more than another twenty seconds now."

In less time than that, the pearl began to melt. Within a few seconds, all that was left of it was some thick red liquid. The spectators gasped in amazement.

Litmus, Bloch, and the gem expert all returned to their seats, and von Himmel continued. "Your honor," he said, "I hope that what you have just seen is enough to acquit Sigmund Kranker of the charge that he still has a stolen pearl in his possession. The pearl that he took from the museum was prepared by Dr. Ph. Litmus and was not a real pearl at all. What Kranker stole, he gave to Ralph Ripoff, who sold it to Mr. Leopold Pancreas — and after a time, it melted. There is no other pearl! Does your honor accept what I say?"

*   *   *

The judge called an hour's recess. When it was over, he began, "I have decided that the accused is not guilty of concealing stolen property. The only charges remaining against him are theft while impersonating Dr. Raphael Bloch, and being an accessory to the kidnapping of Dr. Bloch. The defense may continue with calling its witnesses in connection with these charges."

Von Himmel rose and called Dr. Raphael Bloch back to the witness stand. After establishing that Kranker had indeed impersonated Dr. Bloch, the defense attorney asked Dr. Bloch to repeat what he had said to him the day before.

"Your honor," Bloch began, "I am not learned in the law, but Mr. von Himmel explained a little to me. If I understand him correctly, under the law of this country, a person who has committed a crime cannot be convicted of that crime if the victim of the crime does not press charges but rather forgives him fully. And so, I hereby declare that I have no claims against Mr. Kranker — neither for taking the pearl without my permission, nor for impersonating me, nor even for indirectly helping my kidnappers. To repeat, I have no claims against him."

The defense attorney approached the bench and said, "Your honor, in light of Dr. Bloch's declaration, it is my opinion that the court should cancel Sigmund Kranker's indictment and order him released immediately."

"Your honor, I have something to say!" shouted the prosecuting attorney as he leaped to his feet.

"Yes, Mr. Kutschma?" said the judge, and the prosecutor began. "I agree that it has been established that the so-called

Red Pearl that Sigmund Kranker stole is no longer in existence — and that he therefore should be found innocent of concealing stolen property. Moreover, it is true that the law says that someone who harms another cannot be brought to court unless the injured party sues him. However, that is only as far as monetary damages are concerned.

"Regarding the kidnapping, I believe the court should be severe with the accused, even though Dr. Bloch, the victim of the kidnapping, is standing here whole and healthy — and even though he did not complain to the police about the accused. Kidnapping is a very serious offense, even though the accused did not himself kidnap Dr. Bloch, but only helped those who did.

"I therefore ask," the prosecuting attorney concluded, "that the court find the accused guilty of being an accessory to kidnapping — and give him the maximum punishment for this offense."

Now it was von Himmel's turn. "Your honor!" cried the defense attorney, "the court is not obligated to find my client guilty. In light of all the testimony on the good character of the accused, and in light of Dr. Bloch's full forgiveness, I ask the court to find him innocent and to order his immediate release. Moreover, this trial is not yet over. I have another crucial witness, who will prove to the court that Mr. Kranker's actions were not motivated by greed, but by deep-lying feelings."

The judge called another recess to ponder the matter. When court was back in session, he announced, "I have decided to acquit Mr. Kranker of all charges except the charge of accessory to the kidnapping of Dr. Raphael Bloch. However, he must surrender to the court the money he earned from the robbery and impersonation.

"Regarding the kidnapping charge, on account of Dr. Bloch's refusal to press charges, and on account of the testimony regarding Kranker's good character, I will lighten his sentence if he is found guilty. On the other hand, if I am convinced that emotional reasons drew him into this crime, I will consider acquitting him — especially in light of Dr. Bloch's complete waiver.

"But we are all exhausted and drained. Court is adjourned for the day. We will continue tomorrow morning at nine o'clock."

Everyone in the courtroom stood up, and the judge left.

30

A Surprise Witness

Court started on time the next morning. The spectators became silent and rose when the judge entered.

"I hereby call this court to order," began the judge. "The defense may resume."

The defense attorney rose and said, "Your honor, please permit me to call as witness Dr. Karl von Glick, a Cologne psychologist of long experience."

Dr. von Glick was now a very old man but was still sharp as a tack. He sat in the witness stand and said, "I was asked to give my opinion concerning the accused, Sigmund Kranker, in connection with the charge of his being an accessory to the kidnapping of Dr. Raphael Bloch. I have looked over my records extensively, and I will be able to give you comprehensive report of my conclusions at the time of his treatment.

"When he was a boy, Sigmund Kranker was for a time a patient of mine. His problem was complex and difficult to treat. I believe the root cause of his troubles was that he had lost all conscious memory of his past due to an illness about a year before his parents brought him to me. He wanted very much to know his past, and suffered because he couldn't recall it.

"Because it was so important to Sigmund to recover his past, it troubled him that his parents had no photographs from the years of his childhood — they had all allegedly been destroyed in a fire some time before the boy's illness. From things he said, I could see that unconsciously he longed for a different family — to the point that there gnawed at him the doubt whether the Krankers were his real parents."

The psychologist paused, sighed, and continued. "The fact is, whenever I spoke with Sigmund's parents about his past, his mother became strangely defensive and uncommunicative. It made me wonder sometimes if perhaps the Krankers really were not his biological parents. But it was such a wild idea that I didn't seriously consider the possibility.

"Your honor, Sigmund Kranker and Dr. Raphael Bloch are both sitting before you in this courtroom. You couldn't tell them apart if you didn't know who was who."

"Their resemblance is astonishing," said the judge, "but please get to the point."

"Certainly. Now I will give the court my professional opinion," said Dr. von Glick. "We are talking about a man who has no conscious memories of the first nine years of his life. He wonders whether the man and woman who raised him are his real parents, whether somewhere in the world his real family isn't waiting for him.

"And now, this man is approached by criminals who tell him that in a certain foreign country there lives a man whose resemblance to him is astonishing, even uncanny. The criminals offer to pay him to impersonate this man for a few days, to act as if he were this man. The accused is powerfully driven — one may almost say, compelled — to accept the criminals' proposal by his terrible need to find out about his past and to discover who he really is. He does not accept it because of the money, but because he must know whether or not this stranger who resembles him so closely is a member of the family he thinks he has lost. His overwhelming desire to know his past overcomes all rational and moral considerations and compels him to leap into this adventure."

The aged psychologist returned to his seat. The defense attorney rose and called Kranker to the witness stand.

"Mr. Kranker, did you hear and understand what Dr. von Glick said?" Kranker said he had. The defense attorney continued, "Is it true that you impersonated Dr. Bloch to try to learn about your past, or did you do it for the money?"

Kranker looked at the spectators with piercing eyes, hesitated for a moment, and then said, "First of all, I no longer know whether my name is really Sigmund Kranker, or Moshe Bloch. I began to wonder when I was stung by a bee in my cell."

"A bee?" asked the judge in surprise.

"A bee again?" said Dr. von Glick with a frown.

"Of course a bee!" shouted Raphael and Aharon Bloch together.

"Indeed," said Sigmund, "the moment I was stung by the bee, I felt as if I had been thrown thirty years back in time. Various memories from my childhood blossomed in my head. As I said, I don't know whether I am Moshe Bloch or Sigmund Kranker. My past is not as clear to me as it should be, but it is becoming clearer."

"Excuse me, Mr. Kranker," said the judge, "but you are not answering your attorney's question — which was whether you took part in the theft of the Red Pearl because of the money or because you wanted to impersonate Dr. Bloch for psychological reasons."

"I'm sorry, your honor," said Sigmund. "All I can say is that when one of the gangsters approached me with a proposal to join them in the kidnapping and theft, I was at war with myself. I felt as if something distant and mysterious was pulling me to be Dr. Bloch for a few days. But I don't deny that the amount of money Ralph offered helped me decide in the end to agree to the proposal."

Attorney von Himmel said, "Your honor, at this very moment you can see with your own eyes the emotional whirlpool of which Dr. von Glick spoke. In his psychological turmoil, Mr. Kranker imagines that he is the brother of Dr. Bloch."

"Excuse me, sir!" cried Sigmund. "I am not imagining it! It is not my imagination that makes me think that Dr. Bloch is my brother; it's my memory. I can say beyond a doubt that my name is Moshe Bloch, and that perplexes me terribly — because at the same time I know that my name is Sigmund Kranker!"

Dr. Bloch got up with tears in his eyes and said in a voice choked with emotion, "*Hodu l'Hashem ki tov.* Your memory is beginning to return, Moishy. There never was a Sigmund

Kranker. Your name is Moshe Bloch, and you are our brother, mine and Aharon's." As he said the last words, he pointed to Rabbi Aharon Bloch. He wanted to keep on prodding his brother's memory, but he couldn't speak anymore. Tears rolled from his eyes, and he sat down and sobbed like a child.

The judge looked at the sobbing Dr. Bloch, then at Sigmund — who was as pale as a sheet — then at Rabbi Bloch. "Can anyone here explain to me what is happening?" he said in exasperation. "This trial is turning into a circus!"

Rabbi Bloch spoke from the midst of the spectators. "Your honor, my name is Aharon Bloch and I will explain everything. We were born triplets — I, Dr. Raphael Bloch, and the accused, whose name is really Moshe Bloch and not Sigmund Kranker."

For a moment there was utter silence in the courtroom. Then the spectators all started talking with each other, and the courtroom filled with the murmur of a hundred voices. The spectators were excited by what had been disclosed before their very eyes. "Is it possible?" they asked each other. "The man accused of kidnapping Dr. Bloch is actually his brother?"

At this point, the judge asked if the prosecuting attorney had anything to add.

Kutschma got up with a nasty little smile on his face. "Why yes, your honor, we do. We would like to suggest that what is taking place in this courtroom is deceit and conspiracy. For some reason, Dr. Raphael Bloch and the accused, Sigmund Kranker, want to convince us that Kranker is Bloch's long-lost brother, and was drawn into this crime by his yearning for his real family. But I have proof that the whole thing is nothing but playacting.

"Thanks to reciprocal agreements between Germany and the United States, we were able to subpoena birth records not only for Sigmund Kranker, but for the Bloch brothers as well. They have been faxed to us. They show that Sigmund Kranker was in fact born in Cologne, Germany, in 1951, whereas the Bloch *twins* were born in New York State a year before."

The judge took the faxes and studied them closely. Kutschma, meanwhile, smugly took his place. Pancreas, who a few minutes before had been moving restlessly in his chair, now sat relaxed and smiled to himself in satisfaction.

"Your honor," said the defense attorney, "I am now ready to call my last witness. Do I have the court's permission to summon him?"

"Of course," answered the judge.

The defense attorney whispered something to his assistant, who hurried out of the courtroom. He returned a moment later pushing a wheelchair in which sat an old man.

Sigmund half rose in his chair and exclaimed, "Father!" with emotion, but then slumped back and hung his head in shame at having his father see him sitting in the prisoner's dock.

"Your honor, permit me to call as a witness Peter Kranker, Sigmund Kranker's father.

"Your honor," interrupted the prosecuting attorney angrily, "please forgive my presumption, but can't you see that the accused is trying to mislead the court? Not five minutes ago he said that his name is Moshe Bloch, but just now he called a man named Peter Kranker 'father'."

The judge turned to the defense attorney. "Well, Mr. von Himmel?" he asked.

"Permit me to answer for him, your honor," said a thin voice. With the help of the defense attorney, Peter Kranker came to his feet and stood leaning on the railing of the witness stand.

In a voice shaking with emotion he said, "Your honor, soon you will have to decide whether my Sigmund is guilty of helping the men who kidnapped Dr. Bloch. If you find him guilty, will you give him a lighter sentence because he knew at the time of the kidnapping that Dr. Bloch would be back in his own home in a week's time? Or because Dr. Bloch himself told the court that he forgives him and does not want him to be convicted? Or because the loss of his past caused him great emotional suffering?

"If despite these things you decide to give him the maximum sentence the law allows, then surely you would give an even heavier sentence to someone who kidnaps a person not for a week, not for a month, and not even for a year. No! He was kidnapped for life! He was stolen from his family! And both he and his family suffered terribly because of this. How would this court punish such a crime?"

"Excuse me, Mr. Kranker," said the judge, "but what does that have to do with…"

"Please, your honor, I will explain in a minute. But tell me, what would be the punishment in such a case?"

The judge looked at the frail old man leaning on the railing of the witness stand and decided to answer him. "The maximum sentence for kidnapping is twenty-five years in prison, and…"

Suddenly Leopold Pancreas lurched to his feet, his face ashen, and began pushing his way toward the aisle.

"Your honor!" Peter Kranker cried out in a surprisingly strong voice. "Don't let him get away!"

Pancreas was trembling like a leaf in a storm. The judge looked at him for a long moment and ordered him to return to his place.

Pancreas made his way back and sat down heavily. The policeman who had been standing at the judge's door at the front of the room came and stood in the aisle near where he was seated.

A wave of whispers passed over the courtroom. The judge said, "Mr. Kranker, you are beating around the bush. If you have something to say in your son's defense, say it already!"

"Your honor," said Peter Kranker with both feeling and determination, "I am now going to give testimony in defense of the accused, whom I love very much. With the very same words I will be accusing two people, both sitting in this courtroom, of kidnapping. The first person I accuse is me! I am terribly afraid. Not because I may be punished. Punishment holds no fear for me. Anyone can see that I have one foot in the grave already. No. I am afraid because of someone here in the courtroom, my son, who is so dear to me.

"Thirty-three years ago I saved a young boy from drowning. That young boy was Moshe Bloch. Today he is standing before you in the prisoner's dock, carrying the name Sigmund Kranker. I never thought of keeping the child, but then the devil himself came to my door. The name of this devil is Mr. Leopold Pancreas, who used to call himself Father Pancreas. He started a congregation in our little village in the Catskill Mountains of New York and soon gained our confidence.

"So — this 'respectable' priest drew up a complete plan for me. The main part was the kidnapping of this Jewish boy who had lost his memory because of his near-drowning, and our return to Germany with him. My resistance to this idea was broken by my wife's entreaties.

"This fake priest arranged everything: false documents, the trip to Germany, our first housing — everything. He also saw to it that Moshe's birth was removed from the records in the United States and added to the records in Germany. The German records show that my son Sigmund was born in Cologne.

"So, your honor," exclaimed Peter, "put handcuffs on the real criminals — me and the evil Leopold Pancreas, and leave the wretched kidnapping victim — whom I am ashamed to look in the eye — alone. Let Moshe Bloch finally be reunited with his family!"

All the time that Peter Kranker spoke, Sigmund — Moishy — sat in the prisoner's dock, his whole body shaking. He sobbed noiselessly, but the spectators were horrified.

Peter Kranker hardly had a chance to finish before Pancreas leaped to his feet and shouted, "That's a lie! The whole thing is nothing but a trick! How can you falsely accuse such a respected and important person? How can you say that I forged documents and helped kidnap a child from his parents? I am a proud and law-abiding German citizen!"

Peter Kranker gave Pancreas a look of contempt and said calmly, "Lie as much as you please. As for me, having told the truth, I am at last at peace."

31

It's Never Too Late

In an instant, Kutschma was on his feet. "Your honor, I object to this travesty of justice! Are we supposed to believe the rantings of a sick old man? It is all hearsay, and inadmissible as evidence. I demand that it be struck from the record!"

The judge turned to the defense attorney. "Well, Mr. von Himmel, do you have any proof to back up what Mr. Kranker said?"

"Yes, your honor," answered the defense attorney. "With the court's permission I will present some documents which will prove to be quite revealing.

"We also subpoenaed American birth records — but we demanded the records from the hospital where the Blochs were born and not from the Department of Vital Statistics. We received a fax last night from a hospital in Spring Valley, New York, which states clearly that triplets were born to Shlomo and Chaya Bloch on September 30, 1950. Here is the document for your honor to peruse.

"I also paid a visit to the Bureau of Vital Statistics here

in Cologne. As luck would have it, one of the clerks there is a sixty-year-old man who has been working there for thirty-five years. After I told him who I was — and, uh, threatened to go to the police if he didn't cooperate — he admitted that over thirty years ago he did indeed add a fake birth record to the files. He said that someone had offered him a large sum of money to do it. He even wrote in a fake doctor's name on the birth certificate. Needless to say, I checked the name of the doctor. There never was a doctor by that name in all of Cologne. Here is the clerk's written statement, notarized in my presence."

With those words, von Himmel gave the judge a sheet of paper.

The judge sighed and announced that the court was adjourned until the following morning.

Instantly, the quiet courtroom turned into a stormy sea of voices. Two policemen stood near Pancreas, who was as pale as a corpse.

Sigmund — Moishy, really — cried without stopping. He walked haltingly toward Peter, who sat in his wheelchair, frail and exhausted. When he reached him, Sigmund bent over and took the old man's hands in his own and said, "Father! Beloved father! You saved my life! I forgive you for any wrong you have done me."

Peter Kranker looked at Moishy and said, "I have sinned against you gravely, my son, and even more gravely against your family. And I have also sinned against God. I am old. Soon I will have to give an accounting of all that I have done in this world. There is only one thing that will bring me peace, and I beg of you, Sigmund, do it!"

Sigmund looked at Peter questioningly. Peter continued. "Return to your family! Return to your people! The Creator made you a Jew; I beg of you — return to yourself! Only then will my soul know peace."

Moishy started to say something, but Peter said firmly, "Please, don't say a word. Do as I have asked. Maybe the Lord of Heaven and Earth will forgive me. See, your brothers are waiting for you. Go to them!"

Moishy wiped his tears, looked for a long moment at the frail old man in the wheelchair, and then turned to the where his brothers were waiting.

Raphael and Aharon threw themselves on their brother and embraced him. For a long time they couldn't speak.

"Our Moishy!" Rabbi Aharon Bloch said finally.

Moishy again burst into tears. He couldn't stop. It was as if he were crying for all the years he had lost. Finally, between sobs, he said in a weak voice, "I'm forty-three years old. It's already too late for me."

"Not so!" said Rabbi Bloch. "As long as you are still alive, it's never too late, I assure you. *Kol zeman she-ha-ner dolek, efshar l'takken.*"

Moishy closed his eyes and slowly translated the words in his head. Then he nodded. He opened his eyes and smiled at his brothers.

***Raphael and Aharon threw themselves on their brother and
embraced him.***

32

The End and the Beginning

Now, dear reader, we jump forward ten years. In his small apartment in Haifa, Reb Moshe Bloch had just come home from his *daf yomi* class when the voice of a child was heard asking, "Abba, are you ready to say *Shema* with me?"

"Of course, Shloimy," answered Reb Moshe. He went into his young son's room.

"Abba, when are we going to visit cousin Yossi?"

"Cousin Yossi and his family are coming to us for Purim," answered his father. "Also Uncle Rafi and Aunt Minna."

"Ooh! I can't wait!" exclaimed Shloimy. Then, as he settled down to say the *Shema* he asked, "Abba, are you coming to the Purim party in *cheder*?"

"No, Shloimy, I won't be going. Imma will go."

"Oh, you should come!" chirped the little boy enthusiastically. "There's going to be a magician."

"That," said Reb Moshe with emphasis, "is the reason I am not going."

"But Abba, it isn't magic like what Pharaoh's magicians

did. It's just tricks, like Rebbe Mendel's Wonder Water."

"I know, but I still can't stand magicians. I hope you're not angry with me, sweetheart."

"I'm not angry with you, Abba. But why don't you like magicians?"

"Oh, Shloimy, that's a very long story."

"So tell me part of it before the *Shema*, Abba."

"All right," said Reb Moshe, and he began.

"Far, far away and long, long ago there lived three brothers. One was studious, another was curious, and the third was naughty and a little wild. One day, the naughty brother came into the house red-faced and sweaty and said, 'Areleh, Rafi! Come! I found a donkey on the mountain next to the river.'

"The three brothers went and climbed the slippery hill. At the top they saw the donkey eating the lush grass.

"The wild brother wasn't afraid of slipping on the wet grass and falling down the steep hill, because he was holding on to a big rock. He stood that way for a while watching the donkey.

"Suddenly a bee stung him on the cheek, right by his eye. The boy screamed and let go of the rock. He slipped and tumbled down the hill and fell into the river. He nearly drowned, but a man fishing from a boat on the river saw him fall. The man jumped into the river and saved him, and then took him home and raised him like a son.

"The wild brother forgot his past completely and thought that he was the son of the fisherman.

"Many years passed, and the naughty boy grew up to be

a famous magician in the circus.

"One day, some men asked him to steal a precious stone from his own brother, and the magician, who was the naughty brother, agreed. But in the end, it was this precious stone that brought the naughty brother back to his long-lost family."

"Oh, Abba, you tell such funny stories," Shloimy exclaimed.

Reb Moshe smiled down at the boy and ruffled his hair. "Okay, my sweet boy, it's time to say *Shema*."

Reb Moshe said *Shema* with his son and then kissed his forehead. He sat on the edge of Shloimy's bed as he watched the child fall asleep. "I'm fifty-three years old and my little treasure is only six," he mused. "If thirty-three years of my life had not been stolen from me, I probably would have grandchildren by now like Rafi and Aharon do, and I would know even more of Hashem's sweet Torah. But Aharon is right: as long as one is in this world, it's never too late.

"I thank Hashem for bringing me back, and for giving me a beautiful child to say the *Shema* with every night. *Baruch Hashem* for my wonderful Jewish life."

Glossary of Words and Phrases

The following glossary provides a partial explanation of some of the Hebrew, Yiddish (Y.), and Aramaic (A.) words and phrases used in this book. The spellings and explanations reflect the way the specific word is used herein. Often, there are alternate spellings and meanings for the words.

ABBA: Father, Daddy.

AFIKOMEN: part of the middle matzah that is traditionally hidden during the Passover Seder and then found and eaten at the close of the meal.

AVEIRAH: a sin.

BARUCH HASHEM: "Thank God!"

BERACHAH: a blessing.

BEREISHIS: the Book of Genesis.

B'EZRAS HASHEM: "God willing."

BIRKAS HA-GOMEL: the blessing recited after surviving a dangerous experience.

CHAVRUSA: (A.) a Torah study partner.

CHAZAL: a Hebrew acronym for "Our Sages of blessed memory."

CHEDER: (Y.) a Jewish primary school for boys.

CHIDDUSHEI TORAH: original Torah thoughts.

CHUMASH: [one of] the Five Books of Moses.

DAF YOMI: lit., "a daily page"; a system of studying the entire

225

Gemara during a cycle of approximately seven-and-a-half years, at the rate of one page a day.

DAVEN: (Y.) pray.

ERETZ YISRAEL: the Land of Israel.

GEMATRIA: numerical equivalent; a play on the numerical equivalency of Hebrew words.

HASHIVEINU: lit., "Bring us back," the first word of *Eichah* (the Book of Lamentations) 5:21, which we say when we return the Torah to the Ark.

HODU L'HASHEM KI TOV: "Give thanks to the Eternal, for He is good" (*Tehillim* [the Book of Psalms] 118:1, 136:1).

IMMA: Mother, Mommy.

KAVANAH: concentration.

KERIAS SHEMA: the recitation of the SHEMA prayer.

KITTEL: a white robe worn by men on the High Holidays.

KOL ZEMAN SHE-HA-NER DOLEK, EFSHAR L'TAKKEN: "As long as the candle is burning, it is possible to fix things."

MASECHES: tractate.

MISHLEI: the Book of Proverbs.

MITZVAH/MITZVOS: commandment(s); good deed(s).

NESHAMOS: souls.

PARASHAH: the weekly Torah portion.

PARNASSAH: livelihood.

PESACH SHEINI: lit., a "second Pesach," the fourteenth of the Hebrew month of Iyar, which is a month after the Festival of Pesach. Many Jews have the custom to eat matzah on that day, or to give children promised AFIKOMEN presents.

PILIM: elephants.

POSEK: an authority on Jewish law.

RATZON HASHEM: the will of God.

RAV: a Rabbi.

SABA: Grandfather, Grandpa.

SAFEK: a doubt.

SAVTA: Grandmother, Grandma.

SHACHARIS: the morning prayer service.

SHEMA: "Hear (O Israel)," the opening word(s) of the fundamental Jewish prayer.

SHIUR: a Torah class.

SIFREI KODESH: holy books.

TZADDIK: a righteous person.

TZEDAKAH: charity.

YESHIVA/YESHIVOS: an academy/academies of Torah study.

YIDDISHKEIT: (Y.) Judaism.

ZEMAN KERIAS SHEMA: the proper time for the recitation of the SHEMA prayer.

Glossary of Names

The following list gives you the definitions for some of the names used inside this book. We hope you will enjoy reading it as much as we enjoyed naming the characters. See if you can figure out why we used some of the names.

APFEL: (German) apple.
BONGIORNO: (Italian) "Good morning."
CAPPUCCINO: (Italian) a coffee beverage.
COLITIS: inflammation of the colon.
FELLINI: (Italian) from the word for cat.
(VON) GLICK: (Yiddish) happiness.
(VON) HIMMEL: (German/Yiddish) Heaven.
HOLZWALD: (German) wood forest.
KARISH: (Hebrew) shark.
KRANKER: (German/Yiddish) from the word for sick.
LEO: (French) from the word for lion.
LICHT: (German) light.
LITMUS: a chemical used to indicate acids and bases.
MICHELANGELO: a famous Italian painter.
PANCREAS: a gland in the human body.
PANNO: (Italian) from the word for bread.
PETITE-SOURIE: (French) little mouse.
PH: the measure of acidity and alkalinity in a chemical solution.

(VON) SAUERBRATEN: (German) a marinated roast.

SNAPIR: (Hebrew) fin.

STEINBRECHER: (German) stone-breaker.